THE SHOE BIRD

The Shoe Bird

by

EUDORA WELTY

Illustrated by Beth Krush

UNIVERSITY PRESS OF MISSISSIPPI

Jackson

To Kate and Brookie

First published in 1964
by Harcourt, Brace & World, Inc.
Copyright © 1993 Eudora Welty

Manufactured in the United States of America

The paper in this book meets the guidelines for permanence
and durability of the Committee on Production Guidelines for
Book Longevity of the Council on Library Resources.

Library of Congress Cataloging-in-Publication Data

Welty, Eudora, 1909-
The shoe bird / by Eudora Welty ; illustrated by Beth Krush.
p.   cm.
Summary: Amusing events occur when Arturo, the parrot who works
in a shoe store, fits the other birds with new shoes.
ISBN 0-87805-668-8 (permanent paper)
[1. Parrots—Fiction. 2. Shoes—Fiction.]
I. Krush, Beth, ill.
II. Title
PZ7.W46864Sh 1993
[Fic]—dc20   93-30729
CIP
AC

British Library Cataloging-in-Publication
data available

THE SHOE BIRD

1

There was a certain parrot named Arturo. He worked in a shoe store in the middle of a shopping center in a city in the middle of the U.S.A. Although he had not been born there, the shoe store was his home. It was named The Friendly Shoe Store.

Arturo had a green head, blue wings, yellow eyes, yellow feet, and a yellow tail. His bill was black and shone as brightly as a patent-leather slipper. It was a strong, hooked, and handsome bill, hinged from the top.

Arturo's job might have been hard for some birds, but it suited Arturo exactly. He worked at the right hand of Mr. Friendly, the owner. He helped greet the people coming in. Flying at ladies' elbows or just above children's heads, he escorted them to their chairs. While the clerk tried shoes on their feet, it was up to Arturo to stand by and keep quiet and serious. After that, he flew ahead to perch on the shoulder of the cashier and count along with her when she rang up the sale on the cash register. Back at the door, he assisted Mr. Friendly to send the customers away smiling.

At the close of business hours, Arturo brought a match for Mr. Friendly's pipe, though of course only Mr. Friendly struck the matches. Then, pacing the big old desk, Arturo helped his boss to worry for a short time over his letters and bills.

Even that wasn't all Arturo did, as you'll see.

On a certain fine September day, with a feeling of fall in the air, here came Robbie Thompson, his sister Jane, and his mother, Mrs. Thompson, into The Friendly Shoe Store. Jane came skipping in front, and Robbie came lagging behind.

As Arturo clacked his bright, hinged bill like a door knocker— part of his job—Mr. Friendly said, "Good afternoon, Mrs. Thompson!"

"Come in, Robbie and Jane!" said the Parrot.

"Always glad to see the young people," said Mr. Friendly. "Arturo, please show the Thompsons to three nice seats together." (The Friendly Shoe Store was always jam-packed.)

Arturo escorted Mrs. Thompson, with the children following, to the circle of chairs that ringed the soft, carpeted floor. They sat down. Jane had brought her doll, but as the store was crowded, the doll had to sit on her lap.

"Now, Mrs. Thompson," said Mr. Friendly, "I expect the children have outgrown all their shoes?"

"Indeed they have," said Mrs. Thompson—a young, pretty mother. "And now it's nearly schooltime. I'm afraid both Robbie and Jane need everything."

"Good," said Mr. Friendly. "Arturo, call Mr. Clark, my clerk."

"Oh, Mr. Clark!" called Arturo, flying up the ladder to tap Mr. Clark on the shoulder. In The Friendly Shoe Store, some of the best shoes were placed on the top shelf.

"Mr. Clark, get busy with Robbie Thompson and Jane," said Mr. Friendly. "Try on shoes all day long if you have to. See that these growing feet receive a perfect fit."

"Oh, boy!" said Jane. But Robbie didn't say a word. You might have thought he disliked shopping on a beautiful fall afternoon.

For a long time, Robbie and Jane sat trying on shoes. Mr. Clark was terribly busy with running up and down the ladder to get more boxes from the shelves and hurrying to and fro with shoes about to spill out of his arms. Once he was so anxious to find the right shoe that he dropped a box from the top of the ladder, and when it hit the floor, out popped a pair of giant gum boots, size 12½. And the Parrot kept a perfectly straight face.

It was taking all the beautiful afternoon, thought Robbie Thompson as Mr. Clark laced up his foot in a long brown school shoe. And how hungry he was!

"How is that shoe?" asked Mr. Friendly from the center of the carpet, where he generally stood so he could keep an eye on how everybody was getting along.

"I'm afraid Robbie's toe comes right to the end," said Mrs. Thompson, and Mr. Clark was off up the ladder again.

When it was Jane's turn, everything took twice as long.

"Oh, I could try on shoes all day and all night, too!" she cried, sliding to the floor mirror where she could admire her growing feet in cross-strap patent-leather slippers.

Here is what Mrs. Thompson finally decided on:

For Robbie, brown school shoes, black dress-up shoes, basketball sneakers, and overshoes.

For Jane, the cross-strap slippers, Girl Scout shoes (Brownie size), bedroom slippers of bunny fur, ballet slippers for dancing class, and overshoes.

Mr. Friendly also let Jane pick out a pair of tiny doll shoes for her doll from a box he kept in the drawer in his big old desk. He gave them to her as a present.

"Oh, let's not go home yet," Jane begged her mother. "Could we buy something for Daddy?"

"It's true he hates shopping for himself," said Mrs. Thompson. "But he's never worn the folding Pullman slippers we bought him for his birthday. Still, he does need overshoes."

"I'll see that Mr. Thompson gets a perfect fit," said Mr. Friendly. "That means the largest we have." Arturo handed him a ball-point pen, and he made a suitable memorandum.

"Now the Thompsons will have new shoes from the biggest down to the smallest," said Mrs. Thompson. "My, what an expensive afternoon, but the shoes are worth it!" She gave a check to the cashier, Miss Casey. "Please send everything out in the morning," she told Mr. Friendly.

Arturo was waiting to show them out the door when Jane cried, "Wait!" Her eye had fallen on a revolving table near the window, where a pair of lady's dancing slippers was slowly going round and round. "Mama, when can I wear gold dancing slippers with high heels and diamonds in the toes?"

"When you're as old as I am, perhaps," said Mrs. Thompson with a smile, "and when some lovely invitation comes along."

And as long as they were here in the store, Mrs. Thompson tried on those golden slippers herself, and they were a perfect fit.

"Oh, I wish there'd be a lovely party and I had these to wear!"

she exclaimed. "Somebody will have to have a birthday for that to happen."

So Mr. Clark set the golden slippers back on their table, and they went on turning round.

"Well, good-by now," said Mr. Friendly.

"And come again," said Arturo.

"Good-by, Mr. Friendly, good-by, Mr. Clark, good-by, Miss Casey, and good-by, Arturo," said Jane.

Robbie, up to now, hadn't said a single word. But as he walked out through the door, he turned back and yelled inside: "Shoes are for the birds!"

Robbie's mother bent down and said something into his ear, and they started for home rather quickly.

2

Arturo the Parrot had a motto, and it was this: If you hear it, tell it. He had practiced it all his life long. He was still young, though.

So at the first moment when he wasn't busy at the job, he flew to the window sill and looked out—up and down and in both directions.

The first bird he saw was a Goose.

The Goose, too, was a pet. In fact, she was the pet of Jane Thompson and lived within two blocks of The Friendly Shoe Store. Her name was Gloria. She could fly over the fence.

So Arturo told it to Gloria: "Shoes are for the birds!"

The Goose flew over the fence and came running.

"What grand news!" she cried to Arturo through the window. "Is it a secret?"

"Not now," said Arturo. "My motto is: If you hear it, tell it. But I haven't time for any more now; I'm a busy shoe bird— Yes, Mr. Friendly, I'm coming," he cried.

"I'll *try* that motto," said the Goose, who was a suggestible bird. "It's the first motto I ever heard."

She sped down the street and into the little park at one end of the shopping center.

Four big sycamore trees and a lovely little bandstand stood there. They were left over from the days when the shopping center had been a little village of its own and the park had been the village green. These four old trees changed with the change of seasons, and today was their first day of gold.

In the park, the Goose stopped the first bird she met, a Pigeon.

"Let me tell you what I've just heard!" she cried. " 'Shoes are

11

for the birds!' "

Coming to the park regularly as he did, the Pigeon heard a dozen things every day that later turned out to be rumor, gossip, or wrong information. His eye was round and hard and pink as a little clove.

"What bird told you that?" he asked the Goose.

"The Parrot," she replied.

"He never says anything for himself; he only repeats what somebody else told him," said the Pigeon.

"That way, he's surer to be right," said the silly Goose.

"The question here is, who told the Parrot?" said the Pigeon. "And suppose even just *one* of those two got it backwards? Suppose the correct report is that shoes are *not* for the birds."

"Stop! That would break my heart!" cried Gloria. "If there's anything in the world I can't live without, it's shoes!"

"Have you any idea what shoes are?" asked the Pigeon.

Both Goose and Pigeon had to dodge in and out of shoes everywhere on the feet of shoppers hurrying to the shopping center

and strollers in the park. But they talked right on.

"Shoes? They're prizes," said the Goose. "That's enough for me."

"Have you any idea what a prize is?" asked the Pigeon.

"Certainly I have. A prize is something of great value," she said.

"I'm not sure I'd know something of great value if I saw it," said the Pigeon.

"I'll tell you. A prize is sweet, solid, fluffy and white, and aglow with affection," said the Goose. "It weighs twenty pounds and is given absolutely free."

"Amazing! How is it you know what a prize is when I don't?" asked the Pigeon.

"I *was* one," the Goose replied. "And I must be one still—I haven't changed a jot."

"And somebody got you for nothing?" asked the Pigeon. "Amazing!"

"A prize is *won* by somebody who *deserves* it," Gloria corrected him. "Jane Thompson won me because she deserved me; her father has said so, often. And she had the lucky number to prove it."

"Lucky number? What number is that?" asked the Pigeon. "I might pigeonhole it for my own use."

"One. Or is it one hundred? Or one million? Never mind! Whatever it is, it stands for *me*," said the Goose. "And the Thompsons gave me a home in their back yard with plenty of green grass, where I've been happy ever since."

"Why didn't they eat you?" asked the Pigeon.

"They couldn't," the Goose told him. "They simply couldn't."

"The most amazing part of your story to me is that they got you for nothing," said the Pigeon. "As far as I know, you *can't* get something for nothing. The one exception is popcorn. A Pigeon can get popcorn in the park for no reason except that it's a fine afternoon." And as he spoke, a handful of popcorn was scattered at his feet by a little girl running by. "If you want proof of what I said, have some," he said to the Goose.

"No, thank you," she said. "The Parrot said, 'If you hear it, tell it.' Yet, after telling nobody but you, I feel strangely unsatisfied."

"I'm unsatisfied, too. Tell some more," said the Pigeon. "We birds are to get a prize—but how? Do we just hold our beaks open?"

"For heaven's sake! Don't you know how things are done in the shopping center?" she cried.

"I'm a Park Pigeon," he said. "When day is done, I like to watch the sunset from a bandstand roof, not the top of a parking meter."

"Then I'll tell you," said Gloria. "The Super Supermarket held an Open House in the store. Hundreds of people came! And at the end of the evening, I was led forward and given away with fanfare. Well, the Parrot can do the same thing, and all the birds can come. He can hold Open House in The Friendly Shoe Store, have a lot of fanfare, and give away the shoes. How does that sound?"

"Will it be an event of the fall migratory season?" asked the Pigeon.

"What were you planning to do right away?" asked Gloria.

"As soon as sunset's over, I was going over to the library and dig in," said the Pigeon. That was his home. At the top of one of the big front columns, up in its stone acanthus leaves, he had a dry apartment.

"Well, now you can come to an Open House instead," said Gloria. "We'll round up a wonderful crowd!"

"What birds are you going to invite?" the Pigeon wanted to know.

"Every bird family on earth, I should think," said the Goose. "I'd find it hard to leave anyone out. Of course, some guests we're expecting won't come. And some that we aren't expecting will. I learned that much at the Supermarket."

"You'd better get started with the invitations, then," said the Pigeon. "With so many to invite, you'll have to work fast."

"Can you sing?" she asked. "Sung invitations are sweeter and more far-reaching, too."

"I couldn't carry a tune to save my neck," said the Pigeon. "I coo a little for my own amusement, that's all."

"I can't sing, either. And when I talk too fast, I hiss. And if I hiss my invitations, they'll all fly in the other direction. In a sss-

15

streak!" hissed the Goose.

"Then a messenger had better carry them," said the Pigeon. "It happens I know the very bird you need.

> "For there's not a bit of use
> In arguing with a Goose,"

he cooed to himself as he flew up to the bandstand roof. "I might as well help her."

He cooed two longs and three shorts, his family signal. Down flew his cousin, the Carrier Pigeon.

"If you're scouting around for a message to carry, I've got one for you," said the Park Pigeon, as they walked up and down the little copper roof together. "Here it is: 'Shoes are for the birds.' What do you think of it?"

"Well, it's short and baffling," said the Carrier Pigeon. "Let me try it in code. S.A.F.T.B.," he cooed to himself. "Well, in code it's *long* and baffling. I'll take it."

"Are you sure you know what it means?" asked the Park Pigeon.

"I'll have to crack the code to find out," said the Carrier Pigeon. He stood rolling his eyes, then said, "Well, that was as easy for me as cracking a grain of popcorn is for you. It means that something or other is in store for us birds."

"That's right! In The Friendly Shoe Store," called the Goose, who was listening eagerly from the ground.

"Cousin, tell me what it means in plain Pigeon words," the Park Pigeon kept on. "And repeat it two or three times."

"You want the explanation? You want the interpretation?" asked the Carrier Pigeon. "Well, it's pretty deep. Of course, putting it into code made it deeper still. Carrying a message always makes it twelve times as deep as leaving it in the nest and forgetting about it. I can guarantee this much: by the time I've carried that message all day and brought it home again, you won't know what it meant yourself. Satisfied?"

"Oh, please, couldn't you just say: 'Shoes are for the birds. Open House at The Friendly Shoe Store tonight. Prizes for all,' " begged the Goose. "Instead of explanations and interpretations,

16

just carry them warm *invitations!* Then they'd be more likely to *come.*"

"Whatever you like," said the Carrier Pigeon. "No job's too big or too little for me to handle."

"Then the message is yours to carry for two grains of popcorn," said the Park Pigeon. "You can't get something for nothing, you know."

"Here you are," said the Carrier Pigeon, forking over the popcorn. "Now," he asked the Goose, "do you want this carried to the ends of the earth? That's as far as I go."

"Yes, if there's a bird who lives as far as that from The Friendly Shoe Store," said the Goose. "The Thompsons' back yard is much more convenient for *me.*"

So as he flashed off into blue air, the Carrier Pigeon began to coo to right and left in his soft but carrying voice:

"A mysterious meeting of footling importance to all the birds of the air will be held at The Friendly Shoe Store beginning at sundown. Pass it!"

Of course, this wasn't exactly the invitation the Goose had had in mind. But the Carrier Pigeon cooed to himself, "If I couldn't put a little something of my own into my message, I wouldn't enjoy carrying it."

All over the world, after he'd passed on his way, the birdsong came to be about nothing else. After the Sparrows had cheeped it and the Orioles had warbled it and the Crows had crowed it and the Blue Jays had garbled it and the Hens had clucked it and the Owls were waking up and starting to hoot it, the message got passed further and further on. The invitation was received by Tern and Plover, Nightingale and Swallow, and was passed on— down to the Secretary Bird, out to the Twelve-Wired Bird of Paradise, over to the warm Ostrich, up to the cold Penguin, and on to the ends of the earth where only the Phoenix lives.

"Why, what is this I've been saying?" the Carrier Pigeon asked himself as he made the turn to fly home. "What in the world is 'footling importance'? What are 'shoes'? I think after I get home tonight, I'll accept this invitation myself."

17

3

While the Carrier Pigeon was out carrying the invitations, Arturo was still on the job in The Friendly Shoe Store. He had no idea that as a result of his repeating the words "Shoes are for the birds!" to the Goose, a rather large party was in store for him. He was just a little tired after working at Mr. Friendly's right hand over the last of the day's bills and letters. After talking all day, he was thirsty for buttermilk. So he was glad when closing time came. He flapped up into his little cage.

Mr. Friendly brought him buttermilk and crackers and told Arturo good night.

"Good night, Mr. Friendly. See you in the morning," said Arturo.

Then Mr. Friendly, his clerk Mr. Clark, and his cashier Miss Casey all said a friendly good night to one another. Mr. Friendly saw that the door was locked and the window open to let in plenty of fresh air. He drew the curtain around Arturo's cage last of all. And off they went home.

Pretty soon, the whole shopping center was deserted and calm. The shoppers were gone, the trees in the little park shone, and the copper roof on the bandstand shone, too, in the light of approaching sunset. It was peaceful.

Arturo slept for twenty minutes. Then he opened his eyes, parted the curtains, unlatched the door of his cage with a flick of his bill, flew out, and took charge of the store. For Arturo was also night watchman. Sometimes he stayed awake all night. But at odd moments during the day, he knew how to shut his eyes and nod a time or two, to catch up on his sleep. Arturo was an ambitious Parrot and hoped that by learning all he could about the business, he might win a promotion soon.

Usually, the nights were peaceful and quiet in the store. They grew dark, of course, but Arturo was not afraid, and if the moon should come out, he opened his dictionary and learned a few more words. Once a week the shopping center Cat showed up to check on the mice; that was the only real interruption.

It was sunset. Arturo waked up again—just in time. The first Robin was arriving for the party! He flew into the store by the window, and at his tail flew the Crow.

"Hello, Parrot," said the Crow. "Where's my prize?"

"What's for refreshments?" asked the Robin.

"Refreshments? Prize?" repeated Arturo.

Next the Owl swept in on a gust of air. His eyes were shut, as if he'd flown here in his sleep. And behind the Owl was the Sea Gull, smelling of salt!

The Parrot rubbed his eyes with the tips of his wings. But they were still there. And the next thing he saw was a Peacock!

Luckily, Arturo was a bird who could rise to the occasion very quickly.

"Good evening!" he said. "It's nice to have you all flutter in. I'd have asked you here before now, on my evening off, but supposed you'd all gone to roost."

For Arturo's life was a little lonely. After all, he was the only bird in the store. Mr. Friendly sometimes said Arturo was a bookish bird who needed more exercise. And often, to himself, Arturo had wondered if ever something *would* happen in the shoe store that would help him to know his fellow birds better.

"For heaven's sake!" Arturo now exclaimed. "That's the Secretary Bird who's just arrived! I know her by her picture in the dictionary. She's setting all her hundreds of quills straight, before the mirror. And could I possibly be hearing the voice of the Penguin?"

At that moment the Penguin showed himself at the window, riding on the back of the Ostrich.

"We're not birds of the air; we're birds of the City Zoo," said the Penguin from Ostrich-back. "But may we come in just as home folks?"

"If you have feet, you're always welcome in The Friendly Shoe Store," said Arturo. At once the Ostrich's enormous foot came over the window sill. As he stepped inside, the Penguin turned a black-and-white somersault on his back.

"I'm beginning to wonder," said the Parrot, "if there's any bird in the world who's *not* coming to The Friendly Shoe Store tonight?"

The fact was that all the bird families had safely received their invitations from the Carrier Pigeon. And with only a few hours' notice—in some cases, only a few *minutes'* notice—each family had chosen the best one to send to the party.

The Crow family had sent their loudest Crow, the Owls their wisest Owl. The Peacocks had sent their Peacock with the greatest spread to his tail, and the Swans their most heavenly Swan.

"Come in, Mrs. Quail! Always glad to see the young people," Arturo now said. The Quail had brought four dozen little chicks with her.

"I brought my children because I thought this meeting would be educational," she said. "Well, at least it's deafening."

Can you imagine how noisy it was getting to be inside the store? Not a throat was silent. And the crowd grew larger every minute. The customers' chairs were still standing empty—it was the air that was crowded. Around and around the birds fluttered and flew, as bright as they were noisy, in the last light of sunset.

"There's nothing like old ties," said the Mourning Dove.

"We haven't all of us been together since the Flood!" shrieked the little Wren. "Dear Ostrich, how you've changed."

Now the Park Pigeon arrived. "No bandstand!" he said, looking around. "I'd set my heart on a parade!"

The Blue Jay streaked in. "Hi, everybody! Is this where we're having the prize fights? I'll take on the Mocking Bird!" he cried.

"Parade? Prize fight?" Arturo asked himself. "I'm glad to rise to any occasion—but it would help to know what the occasion *is.*"

Then here came the Goose.

"Isn't this lovely?" she cried, waving, as she cleared the window sill and fluttered into the thick of them all. She wore the blue ribbon she'd worn when she was first prize at the Supermarket.

"Thank goodness the Goose is here," said the Parrot to himself. "She looks as if she knows more about this occasion than anybody."

Instead of letting her family go to the trouble of picking out their most foolish—it might have taken them months—Gloria had volunteered to be it herself. Her family had agreed that since she'd

thought up the party, she deserved the honor.

"How soon will the prizes be given out, Parrot?" she cried. "But how surprised you look!"

"Oh!" exclaimed Arturo. "Why didn't I think of that? Of course! This is a surprise party. Then it must be my birthday!"

"Don't you know whether it's your birthday or not, sir?" asked the forty-eight little Quails. It was not *their* birthday, and they knew it.

"I would have to fly to Patagonia and ask my mother, to be sure," said the Parrot. "That's where I was born, several years ago. By the time I found out and flew back here, you might all have got tired waiting and flown home. And I'd have missed everything. It's not every night that a Parrot gets taken so completely by surprise."

"What?" cried Gloria. "Didn't you get my invitation to your Open House?"

"I don't believe I did," said Arturo. "Did it come in Mr. Friendly's mail with the rest of the circulars?"

"It should have come by Carrier Pigeon," said the Goose. "I see he hasn't got back yet. I expect he was saving your invitation for last. Never mind! You're *here*."

"I'm always here," said Arturo. "Though it's never been like this."

"Well, tonight you're holding Open House," the Goose said.

"I don't know what an Open House is. I'd feel more sure of myself thinking it was a surprise party," said Arturo.

"I don't know what a surprise party is," said the Goose.

"It's very surprising," Arturo said. "Last night, after business hours, Mr. Clark and Miss Casey gave Mr. Friendly, our boss, a surprise party and a surprise."

"But *everything's* a surprise," interrupted the Goose. "Only prizes are really worth giving—to those who deserve them."

"Well, you might have called Mr. Friendly's surprise a prize," said Arturo doubtfully.

"I can soon tell you. Was it beautiful?" asked the Goose.

"Yes," said Arturo.

"Was it white and fluffy?"

"That's right."

"Was it aglow with warmth and affection?"

"It was all aglow," he said.

"It sounds like a prize, all right," said the Goose. "And was it heavy?"

"It was a little heavy, though Miss Casey said she'd hoped it wasn't," said the Parrot.

"Well, it's not every prize that can weigh twenty pounds, I expect," said Gloria. "But I'm sure Mr. Friendly's prize was just like me."

"Then your icing didn't stick," said Arturo.

"Shouldn't we invite Mr. Friendly's prize to the party?" asked the Goose.

"We can't. He ate it," said Arturo.

"He ate it?" cried Gloria. "He ate his prize?"

"It was a birthday cake," explained the Parrot. "With dozens of candles on it, all aglow. Miss Casey had baked it at home till it was light and fluffy and swirled white icing all over it, and put his name on top in red icing. Mr. Friendly blew out the candles, Miss Casey sliced it, and they all gobbled it up. They gave me a piece. I pecked at it, out of politeness."

"I simply could never eat a prize myself," said the Goose. "We'll have better manners than that here tonight. You said you gave the prize to Mr. Friendly at his surprise party. That was doing things backwards—the Pigeon says that's easy. Why in the world didn't Mr. Friendly give the prize to you?"

"Mr. Friendly said at the time that he didn't deserve it," Arturo said. " 'I don't deserve a beautiful gift like that!' " he said.

"He certainly did not deserve it if he ate it," said the Goose.

"If I'd wished to eat something I didn't deserve, I'd have called for a banana," said the Parrot.

"A *banana?*" asked the tiny Hummingbird.

"A *banana?*" asked the Sea Gull.

"Parrot, who *are* you?" they asked.

"My name is Arturo. They call me the shoe bird," he said.

"Shoe bird? What's that? What's *shoe* mean?" asked the Crow. "Is that something you eat, too?"

"Certainly not. Shoe can mean either of two things," said Arturo. "One shoe is what is worn on the feet. And the other shoe is a word you say to make something fly away. I certainly hope you know which kind of shoe bird I am."

"We are glad to meet you," they said.

And the Penguin said, "Shoo!"

"Don't!" cried Arturo. "Everybody hold on tight!" he warned. "You can blow away at a word like that!"

"I was only joking. I take it back," said the Penguin.

"The meanings of words are serious things, you know," Arturo said as he settled on the desk.

"Well, we don't have to worry about words," said Gloria the Goose. "We've got prizes coming. And I hope, Parrot, that you have enough to go around."

"I!" he cried. "Arturo?"

"Who else?" she cried back.

"But I have nothing at all! I'm only a shoe bird, working days and nights in hope of early promotion," Arturo said.

"Oh, yes you have got something," said Gloria excitedly. "You must give a prize to every single bird here!"

"I've heard a lot of talk tonight about prizes and surprises," said Arturo. "But I didn't realize I had any. What can they be? Let's see. A prize is meant to be given away. A surprise is *not* meant to be given away, but the best surprises are. So whatever it is, it's a gift. Now—what gift have I got to give?"

"Don't you know?" cried the Goose. "It's pretty late to be wondering, with everybody waiting!"

"I'm afraid I never know unless I'm told," said Arturo. But all at once, he felt impatient with that idea. "Why yes, I was born with the gift of words," he said. "I study words on the job and in my spare time by myself. I've already learned Commercial English; I've installed a dictionary in my private office. How would you like me to give you some Shakespeare one of these days?" he asked the Goose.

"Shakespeare won't do," said the Goose. "But you're getting warm, because the prize does begin with an s-s-s-s-s."

"Suet?" Arturo guessed. "No, there's nothing here in my sau-

24

cer but the usual buttermilk and crackers. For a crowd this size, that would hardly go farther than the Robin. And some of these birds would expect fish.''

''The prize is not Shakespeare; the prize is not suet; if you can guess any closer, I wish you would do it,'' said Gloria.

''Give me one hint,'' said Arturo. ''I think that's fair.''

''All right. All you have to do is remember something you said yourself,'' said the Goose. ''That shouldn't be hard.''

''It's harder than you know,'' Arturo said. ''I'm speaking words all day long, and sometimes I practice them at night alone, when I'm enjoying flights of fancy. I bet I've already repeated as many words in my life as there are stars in the sky, and I'm only three years old today, if today's my birthday. So it would be very hard for me to pick out just the words you mean out of all I've spoken.''

''It's SHOES!'' the Goose gaily cried. ''Don't you remember now? You announced this morning from that window: 'Shoes are for the birds!' Those were your words, and here are the birds. *We've all come!*''

The Parrot in his amazement rose to the chandelier. And flying, flying, everywhere around him were all his unexpected, his terribly excited, guests.

''If you hear it, tell it,'' he gasped to himself. ''And if you tell it, you may have a surprise party before the sun goes down!''

4

Would you believe it that all this time the Owl had been asleep?

Now he woke up and said, "What's all the excitement? I'd like an account of what's been going on here." He cleared his throat with a hoot. "Then I'll give you my opinion on it, which I can see is badly needed."

"Oh, please let's have prizes before opinions!" cried the Goose. "It's so much luckier that way." And before the Owl could say it wasn't, she'd pranced to the top of the shoe stool. "If the prizes are ready, we are!" she cried. "Parrot, start giving away the shoes!"

The birds went wild to hear her, flapping and clapping with their wings and giving loud whistles.

"I'd have to take Mr. Friendly's place to give away the shoes," Arturo said to himself. "But I don't think he'd mind—he never warned me not to."

So Arturo got out of the chandelier, glided to the floor, and took up the usual position of Mr. Friendly during business hours, patting his foot in the center of the carpet.

The birds went wild again. They soared to the ceiling. Some of them flew around the room going sixty miles an hour. Arturo clacked his beak for quiet. It sounded like a ruler being rapped on the teacher's desk.

"Stop flying, right where you are!" he yelled, for how could shoes be fitted on feet with the customers flying around in the air? Could Mr. Friendly himself do that without a stout pair of wings on his back? Arturo doubted it.

"Be seated!" he yelled. "As far down from the ceiling as possible!"

Down they settled, all at the same instant. And if you had happened to look in through the window of The Friendly Shoe Store at that moment, this is what you would have seen:

There was an Owl on the hatstand. There was a Sea Gull on the water cooler. There was a Woodpecker on the typewriter, a Secretary Bird at the telephone. Sparrows were lined up along the cord. (If one Sparrow was invited anywhere, the whole flock always came.) A Pigeon stood on Mr. Friendly's desk, in a pigeonhole. A Crow perched at the smoking stand, pretending to be smoking, and a Peacock had found the floor mirror. And the chairs were occupied now. The whole circle was wound around and around with rows and rows of birds, like tier upon tier at the Opera House. And there was the Goose presiding on the shoe stool, with her eyes sparkling, as if she were just ready to become an opera star.

And now, exactly as in the Opera House before the curtain goes up, everything went dark. The sun had set. And of course no lights came on inside.

The birds, who'd been ready to sing, began: "Give us our shoes! Give us our shoes! Give us our..."

And then their song ran down.

The birds began to yawn. Hundreds of bird beaks opened in yawns of every size. The birds were about to go to roost where they sat!

"You'll have to wake up," cried Arturo. "I can't promise you a perfect fit in shoes without your cooperation." He flew back to the chandelier and tinkered with it with his bill, but he was no electrician, and since he didn't know how to push the button, the lights didn't come on. The store grew darker and darker.

But of course this was also the hour when the Owl began opening his eyes. First one eye, then both eyes opened wider and wider. His big yellow globes lighted the store from top to bottom, and now you could see all the other birds waking up again, just as at sunrise, and Arturo himself hanging by one nervous claw from the chandelier.

"—so give us, oh, give us our shoes!" sang the birds. They took up their song where they'd left off, as birds do after night has passed over, or a little shower of rain.

So Arturo took a deep breath and called, "Mr. Clark? Mr. Clark?"

At first, there was no answer. (The real Mr. Clark was having supper with Miss Casey in her little apartment ten minutes' walk from the shopping center. This time, she'd cooked a pineapple upside-down cake.)

"Who will be Mr. Clark?" asked the Parrot. "If Mr. Friendly needs Mr. Clark, I do too."

"I will," the Goose volunteered. "Only for this evening, though. Don't expect me to forget that I'm really a Goose." She took a slide down the slope of Mr. Clark's stool and asked, "How was that for a start?"

"Pretty good. And now climb up to the top of the ladder, pick out the shoe box that's at the bottom of the tallest stack on the highest shelf, then drop it," directed the Parrot. "After that, you'll learn as you go along."

The Goose tripped over to the ladder and up it. Using her long white neck, she swung at the top shoe box and sent it to the carpet like an expert. There sat a shoe box on the floor, at the birds' feet.

For the first minute or two, it wasn't touched.

Then, "Is it hollow?" cried the Woodpecker, sailing for the box and going to work on the lid to make a hole in it.

The Oriole was there, warbling, "Tissue paper! Tissue paper! Just what I need to make my nest more nestlike." And she ripped off with a long streamer.

The Robin tugged two brown shoestrings out and swallowed them both. "They tasted stringy," he said. "But I only tried two. I might like the third one better."

The Goose had burrowed her head in under the lid and under the paper. As her long, sensitive neck, and also her tail, quivered with excitement, she dug something out.

"Well, look what I've unearthed!" she exclaimed.

There on the carpet stood a boy's brown school shoe with its lace gone.

"Is that nest open to the public?" cried the Cuckoo, at once on the wing. "If so, I'm anxious to claim it."

"Just a moment!" The Parrot clacked his bill again for attention. "That is a SHOE."

"You don't mean it. Is *that* a shoe?" cried the Goose. "Why, as a prize it can't compare with me! Fly back a little," she warned the other birds. "It may not even be affectionate! What will they hatch out next in the shopping center!" And she said to Arturo, "There never was a prize like that!"

"There's another one just like it in the same box," said Arturo. "But perhaps I should explain about shoes. You birds may not appreciate what we call the merchandise. Do you know what to do with a shoe?"

The Cuckoo, the Curlew, the Emu, and a rather odd bird called the Curlicue led the birds in a chorus, singing:

"Who can tell us, who?
What can birds do with a shoe?
Oh, who?"

"Well, I'm a shoe bird," Arturo began. "I may be who."

But a deeper voice than his, speaking from the hatrack, said "Hoot! I'm an Owl. I'm who!

"A shoe box," the Owl went on, "is not made *primarily* to peck holes in. The tissue paper in the shoe box is not made *primarily* to line nests with. And the shoelaces in shoes are not made *primarily* to be gobbled up for worms. The shoes that come out of shoe boxes are not made *primarily* to be used as cuckoos' nests. Neither do shoes come from eggs."

"I'll always remember it, every word," said Arturo. "But how do you know so much, Mr. Owl? After all, you live in a tree."

"I know it because I have the gift of wisdom," replied the Owl. "I'll even give a demonstration of what shoes are for."

He swooped down and picked up a pair of shoes from the desk— the doll shoes. He shoved them up onto his ear tufts. The toes stuck up, and their small buckles winked in the light of the rising moon, which at this moment began to look in through the window, brighter than his own yellow eyes.

"Shoes are to wear," he continued. "Thus!" And he modeled the shoes on his ears. He turned his head to left and right. "But since most of you have only indifferent ear tufts, compared to mine, you'll have to wear your shoes like people—on your feet."

"What if the shoes are too big?" asked the Hummingbird. "Hummingbirds have such tiny feet that some say we haven't any."

"I have given you all the benefit of my wisdom. I have shown you by my example. But I am not open to questions," said the Owl.

First one eye, then the other, shut down. (But luckily, the moon went on shining.) The ruffles of his feathers rose and fell, soft as chiffon. The wise Owl went back to sleep. Perhaps the shoes on his ears shut out the noise that all the other birds made now.

"We want shoes!" they cried. "We want shoes on our poor little feet!"

"Then, will you once more have the kindness to be seated?" asked Arturo, for the birds were all up in the air again!

After they'd settled, he said to the Goose, "Now, Mr. Clark has a certain motto. I don't like it as well as mine, but here it is: 'If at first you don't succeed, try, try again.' That's how he fits shoes."

"All right, I'll try 'Try, try again,' " said the Goose, and scrambled up the ladder for a new box.

She poked her head in so eagerly, trying so hard, that every shoe box in the store promptly fell down, and shoes tumbled out right and left, all over the carpet.

"Now you're learning," Arturo called to encourage her.

"Why, there's a million shoes! That's enough to give a prize to every bird in the world, even two to a bird!" cried Gloria.

"And now, Mr. Clark," Arturo told her, "you have our complete line at your disposal, a wealth of styles that are up-to-the-minute and very pretty to choose from. So please see to it that these tiny feet receive a perfect fit."

"If I can't do that, I'll have a perfect fit myself," the Goose promised.

5

The Goose brought out a man's overshoe first, and she tried a Sparrow's foot in it. What happened to the Sparrow? It went out of sight. So she tried again, by adding another Sparrow. The same thing happened. Then one Sparrow more. Out of sight!

"You're just throwing good Sparrows after bad," said the Crow rudely.

The Goose hated to give up. She tried the whole flock of Sparrows, and they all fell in. Indeed, this overshoe was one of the largest pairs in the store, and had been tagged "Mr. Thompson, Urgent."

"It just seems to be too big all over," cheeped the little Sparrows.

"I'm afraid you won't do," said the Goose kindly. "I'll try a larger bird in the next shoe."

With her long neck she beckoned to the Ostrich.

"But I don't need overshoes. I'm planning to leave the Zoo and go home to the desert," said the Ostrich. "That's all dry sand."

"You never know when it will rain, turn cold, and freeze over," the Goose replied. "Your foot, please."

So the Ostrich put out his foot, and the overshoe disappeared.

"Why, your feet are the wrong size too!" exclaimed the Goose. "If I were you, Ostrich, I'd go back to the desert and hide my big feet in the sand!"

She went for another pair of overshoes and came back with them, pushing each one in front of her, like a nurse with a baby carriage. This time, she tried the Sea Gull.

"I like these, and I like their squeak," he said. "But they're as big on my feet as the *Queen Mary*." That was the ocean liner the Sea Gull had met that morning as she sailed into New York Harbor.

The Goose was trying hard. She was trying even harder than Mr. Clark, for it is harder to find a foot to fit a shoe than to find a shoe to fit a foot. Especially, of course, a bird's foot. "Nobody fits!" she said at last. "Oh, dear me."

What would Mr. Friendly do now? Arturo wondered.

"I think there's a sale coming up," he announced.

"A sail? A sail coming up on the horizon of the shopping center?" cried the Sea Gull. "Then I must fly to meet it at once, to welcome it with harsh cries."

"If you used the dictionary—" the Parrot said, and he was turning the pages of his, very fast.

"I don't," said the Sea Gull.

"I do," said Arturo, "and it hasn't taken me long to find out that some words mean two things. Now, you're a thousand miles off about sale. That's how far off the ocean is from the shopping center, by the way. My kind of sale is a business word."

"My kind of sail is a sea word and a sky word and a wind word," said the Sea Gull. "It's a word out of history. Almost as long as there have been Sea Gulls, there have been sails. My forefathers flew to meet the Phoenician sailboats and welcomed them with harsh cries."

"I'm interested to learn that," said Arturo, "but I must get back to business here." Now he went to Mr. Friendly's desk and opened the drawer and took out the Sale sign. It said, "Sale! These Shoes Are Reduced."

"Tack that to the post, young fellow," he told the Woodpecker. "And now try that shoe again," he told the Goose. "I think you'll find it's a little nearer the right size."

The shoe was smaller now, but the Sea Gull said, "It's still too roomy for my foot."

"We can reduce it a little more," said Arturo. He pulled the second sign out of the drawer, and the Woodpecker tacked it up— "Shoes Greatly Reduced."

"That's better—keep on," cried the Sea Gull.

Then they kept reducing them more and more, until at last they put up a sign that said "FINAL REDUCTION."

"Wait! They're gone altogether!" screeched the Sea Gull.

"They almost took me with them!"

So the Parrot quickly took down the "Final Reduction" sign and as he shut it back up in the drawer, the overshoes gently slid back into view. And when the Sea Gull tried again, he was a perfect fit—as if he'd been made for the overshoes in the first place.

"Parrot, what made you so clever?" asked the Goose.

"I'm not really clever," said the Parrot honestly. "But I hope to make the most of the brains I have. Have you ever thought of trying that?"

"Never in my wildest dreams," she declared.

"I study words," Arturo said. "That's why I keep a little dictionary in my office, on a little dictionary stand—you may have noticed me looking in it a time or two tonight. I just looked up 'reduce.' It means to lower the price, as Mr. Friendly knows. But it has seventeen other meanings too—even 'to crush to powder.' Isn't that wonderful? But I was looking for something not quite as strong as that. So the meaning I took was 'to make smaller in size.' So that's what happened when I reduced the shoes."

"Not bad," said the Owl, opening his eyes. "Not bad at all, for a Parrot. How did you get such a tiny little dictionary?"

"Oh, dictionaries come in bird size," said Arturo. "If I were an Owl, I'd go in a bookstore and browse."

"I do," said the Owl.

After this, the Goose's work ran smoothly. Soon, almost all the shoes in The Friendly Shoe Store were successfully fitted onto the feet of the birds.

"I'll be careful not to reduce Mr. Thompson's overshoe in the excitement," Arturo said. "Just go around it, everybody. It's sheltering a whole flock of Sparrows, and I wouldn't want to disturb it."

As she stood on tiptoe atop the shoe stool, the Goose saw the brightest thing of all. Those golden slippers on the little table, down below her, were going around and around. They went spinning before her vision, and with their paste diamonds sparkling they were nearly as bright as her eyes were.

"I see the grand prize!" she cried.

"Where? Where?" And they all crowded around the table to see. It was the Penguin who flipped the golden slippers to the floor and began stuffing his big cold feet inside.

"Ssssstop, ssssssir!" hissed the Goose, sliding down the stool like a streak. "The grand prize has to be given away last! The lucky number will get those golden shoes. Just look, your feet have frozen the diamonds to pure ice. Aren't you ashamed?"

"I'll never do it again as long as I live," promised the Penguin. "I was only clowning."

After this, there was pretty good order in the store. And the Goose worked so fast that she seemed to be everywhere at once.

"I only hope we have enough birds for all the shoes, so we'll come out even," she said. "It would be a pity to have prizes left over."

"Do you look for any unexpected guests?" asked Arturo.

"Oh, yes. It would hardly be an Open House without a few unexpected guests arriving," said the Goose, and at that moment one arrived.

"Nobody gave me a special invitation," said the Whippoorwill, "though I waited as long as I could. Then, on my way, I was delayed by tears. I had to wade through all my tears to get here."

"How sad you sound this evening," said the others.

"I sound sad every evening, if you'd only pay attention," said the Whippoorwill. "What is this occasion? Is there anything going on to make me wish I'd stayed home?"

"It's an Open House," said the Goose.

"To me, it's a surprise party," said the Parrot.

"To me, it's a family reunion," said the Dove.

"To me, it's a P.T.A. meeting," said the Mother Quail.

"My invitation said it's a mysterious meeting of footling importance. And I agree," said the Sea Gull, as he walked up and down in his rather squeaky overshoes.

"May I be president?" asked the Whippoorwill. "I think you ought to make me president of whatever it is, if only to keep me from crying."

"No, because everybody would rather hear you crying than vote for you," said the Owl.

"Oh, sad! Oh, sad!" said the Whippoorwill. "Not one vote for poor Will?"

"Stop crying long enough for me to try you in a pair of Wellington boots," said the Goose kindly. "Maybe they will help you through your tears on the journey home."

"Since I'm so sad, wouldn't something a little grander be better for me?" complained the Whippoorwill. "Something with tassels?"

But it did him no good to complain, for his sopping feet were the perfect fit for the Wellington boots, once they'd been reduced and turned down in cuffs. There he stood in them, sobbing—breaking them in by getting them wet with tears.

"Now, who's this coming?" asked the Goose. "This guest is not only unexpected—he's a total stranger."

The stranger bird came toppling in over the window sill and landed with a crash on the floor.

"I wasn't invited at all," he said after he was steady on his feet. "I am a Clay Pigeon, and please forgive me for coming in this way. I work at the Shooting Gallery in the Amusement Park on the other side of town. I've come all this way to ask: Is there a shoe that might keep me from going to pieces every night on the job?"

"I think I can do something for you," said the Goose. "Here is a good, black, oil-tanned, oak-grained leather shooting boot with rawhide laces. It's the very shoe you need, in a loose fit. I recommend that you stay 100 per cent inside it."

"Thank you," said the Clay Pigeon.

"You seem to have caught onto the shoe business remarkably well, Goose," said the Owl when the Clay Pigeon had clattered out with his new shoes hung by the laces around his neck. "But you don't know much about your fellow birds. That stranger was not a real Pigeon."

"But he was in real trouble," the Goose pointed out. "I'm glad we helped him. Now, is this a *third* unexpected guest?"

The Twelve-Wired Bird of Paradise was flying in.

"Have we met to elect the most glorious of birds?" he asked. "I've flown all the way from New Guinea, in case it's me." And he had brought a wreath of bird's-foot violets, feathered carnations, eglantine, and seed pearls.

"Did you bring that all the way from New Guinea to be crowned in? There's one just like it in the shopping center. You could have picked it up at the hat bar in the chain store," said the Goose, who was a window-shopper. "But you look very nice without a wreath."

"Oh, I must look terrible! Everything I have is last year's," the Twelve-Wired Bird of Paradise replied in modest tones. "Just look at these old feathers. And I haven't been tuned since the Flood."

"You look and sound fit as a fiddle," the Goose assured him. "I see only one thing lacking in your appearance—you have no shoes. Let me give you a perfect fit."

"All right. Just a modest little shoe. Just something that goes with what I already have on," he replied.

What surprised the Goose, then, was that every shoe she brought out to him was the wrong thing.

"Me wear that? Imagine!" he'd cry. And she'd have to try, try again.

"It's hard to draw the line where moulting and modesty leave off and vanity begins," said the Goose to herself. "The Twelve-Wired Bird of Paradise may be modest, as he says he is, but I believe he's got his eye on those golden slippers!"

Of course she didn't try those on him. "The lucky number gets the grand prize," she said again.

At last, the Twelve-Wired Bird of Paradise consented to wear some velvet opera boots lined with ermine, after they had been reduced to almost nothing.

"Sir, would you care for shoes on your feet as well as your ears?" the Goose asked the Owl.

"My dear Goose," he replied, "I can't help it if I look a little odd and eccentric, you know. I am happier with shoes on my *ears*. Indeed, you will have to show me a shoe with a toe that will turn round and round, like *my* toe, before I will wear them anywhere *except* on my ears.''

''This is the nearest thing I have,'' said the Goose, drawing some Pullman slippers out of their case. They were soft and red and flexible, like gloves, and the Owl tried his feet in them. But he shook his head.

''I can't picture myself trying to wear these and eat a mouse at the same time,'' he said. ''I suppose I'm set in my ways.''

''You may keep shoes on approval and return them in ten days, if unworn,'' said Arturo. ''Your money will be cheerfully refunded, with no questions asked.''

''They have a strange effect of making me sleepy,'' said the Owl and, still wearing the Pullman slippers, drifted back to sleep on the hatstand.

''But Parrot! What about yourself?'' all the rest of the birds began to sing. ''What about *your* shoes?''

How Arturo had hoped his own feet would go unnoticed! He had always worked barefooted; still, Mr. Friendly did otherwise.

''Well, nothing for it now but for me to step into these,'' he said to himself, and he stepped into shoes that he believed were exactly like those Mr. Friendly wore. They were brown crocodile, reduced.

The fact was, though, that Mr. Friendly wore the most ordinary brown oxfords, which he kept beautifully polished. The brown crocodile shoes just stood for a mistake on Arturo's part.

''Well, Goose,'' said Arturo, patting his foot in these, ''you must be next. Now, shoe yourself.''

''Hooray!'' Gloria cried. ''Well, here comes the announcement everybody's been waiting for. Who gets the grand prize? Who is the lucky winner of the golden dancing slippers with diamonds in the toes? It's me!''

''The Goose gets the grand prize!'' the Oriole warbled, and the Vireo, the Indigo, and an unusual bird called the Yoyo joined her to lead the chorus as they sang:

''Surprise! Surprise! The Goose herself gets the prize!''

''Wait a minute. I thought you said the lucky number would get the grand prize,'' complained the Twelve-Wired Bird of Paradise. ''Well, I'm 12. What are you?''

''You may say it's one; you may say it's one million. Whatever

it is, it's me," said the Goose. "I'm the living lucky number, the living grand prize, Gloria Goose. And so the golden slippers are mine!"

She set her foot up onto the little revolving table (which never stopped) and up she went. She slipped her own yellow feet into those slippers of gold. She rose up four inches in those high heels. There she posed.

"To get a prize, *be* a prize!" she cried.

And around she went. She rode around and around, twenty times at least, before she stepped back down to the carpet. If this had made her any dizzier, nobody could tell it.

"Congratulations!" Arturo said to her. "Would you like to sit still long enough for me to give you a better fit?" For her shoes were still size 6½B—exactly Mrs. Thompson's size.

"No, I don't want a thing about me changed," the Goose replied.

And she walked around in them like that the whole evening long.

"Oh, but these are neat," she said.

6

"Did I hear you say, 'To get a prize, *give* the prize'?" the Park Pigeon asked the Goose.

"Of course not. I said. 'To get a prize, *be* a prize,' " the Goose corrected him.

The Owl woke up just as though an alarm clock had gone off in his ear, right through the doll slipper. "What bird is spouting wisdom in here besides me?" he asked.

"It is I," said the Goose. "But I didn't mean to spout wisdom, I was only saying in plain words how I happened to get the golden slippers. I simply deserved them." And she drew one slippered foot behind the heel of the other and took a bow.

"I'd appreciate it if you'd leave all the wise remarks to me," said the Owl. He still looked a little ruffled.

"Hey! Now that we've all got shoes on, what do we do next?" asked the Crow.

"We break them in," said the Goose. "By walking."

"*Walking?*" they chorused.

And the Oriole asked in song, "Haven't all birds *dreamed* of walking? Of getting where we wanted to go *slowly?* Of coming down out of the clouds one day to solid earth?"

Most of the birds said yes, although the Crow said he'd dreamed more often of driving a motorcycle, and the Dove began to tell her dream of falling.

"Never mind. Just get in formation behind me, and we'll start," said Gloria.

"Where'll we go?" they asked.

"Around and around," said the Goose. "Around and around the store in our nice new shoes. Haven't you ever gone in circles?

I have, and there's no other feeling like it."

"Suppose we want to hop?" asked the Robin. "I'm a hopper."

"Hop ahead, just so you don't hop out of your nice new shoes," the Goose said. "How would I ever get everybody fitted all over again?"

"I never knew I *could* walk," the tiny Hummingbird said. She took one step and told them in faint tones, "I feel funny."

"Take deep breaths and don't tuck your head under," advised the Sea Gull. "It's the unaccustomed stillness of the floor under foot. It's so solid and so still. When the wind blows, this floor stays right where it is. Be careful."

But she staggered again.

"A drop of nectar, please—quickly!" she gasped.

"I haven't any nectar," said the Parrot anxiously. "Will buttermilk do as well?"

She shook her head. So he brought the bottle of smelling salts from the bottom desk drawer where Miss Casey kept it. (Miss Casey fainted at the sight of mice.) He held this to the Hummingbird's quivering beak until she said she felt well enough to go on.

So the Goose led off. And they all walked in their shoes behind her. The crowd on the floor was as bright as the crowd in the air had been, earlier. Only it moved nothing like sixty miles an hour. At first, it hardly seemed to move at all.

"It's a parade!" said the Park Pigeon. "It's the way a parade always starts. I don't suppose Mr. Friendly keeps a steam calliope on hand?"

"Yes, it's called Muzak," said Arturo. "It plays for the whole shopping center. But when it's time for the stores to close, the Muzak dies away."

"Listen! I hear music all the same," said the Oriole.

Here came the Sandpiper, piping tunes on the shoehorn. And as the Canary whistled, the Woodpecker rapped in 14/16 time on a shoe-box lid, and the Starling beat with alarming loudness on an ash tray with one of Miss Casey's hatpins for a drumstick. Some Hawaiian bird strummed a strange instrument made entirely of rubber bands. The Twelve-Wired Bird of Paradise vibrated and gave off a harplike sound that was somewhat electrifying. The rest of the birds contented themselves with singing.

Arturo himself took his place in the center, so that the parade could march around him. He patted his foot in its crocodile shoe, and before long he began to clack his bill in delicate rhythm. It was the Patagonian coming out in him.

The Hummingbird had got the feel of the floor now. Her boots were drum majorette boots. They looked like two small white florets from the earliest hyacinth, prancing their way along the carpet. She whirred with her wings to add to her performance— but of course her wings couldn't lift her off the ground so long as she had her boots on.

"I've heard the old human saying, 'Keep both feet on the ground,'" remarked the Owl, shuffling along in his Pullman slippers and wagging his doll shoes. "But I never realized before how people managed to do it. *Their shoes are ballast.*"

The heavenly Swan stood against the wall and practiced toe stands in the ballet slippers she wore, but all the rest of the birds were out in full swing now. The Peacock held his blue neck tall and waltzed about on his toes in slippers of peacock-blue velvet. With an occasional forward sweep of his tail, he lightly strummed the small lyre that crowned his head and accompanied his own shrieks of joy. The Dove kept time by stamping in her nurse's shoes. And the Sea Gull took to the air, once, with his overshoes raised high, feet wide apart, toes turned up—and soared like a Russian dancer over all their heads, to alight on the telephone. It was almost like flying!

In his black basketball sneakers, smoking a cigarette from the smoking stand, the Crow advanced to meet the Scarlet Tanager, and wing laid on wing they performed an Apache dance.

The Parrot went into Miss Casey's drawer again and this time got her comb. He spread a little piece of tissue paper over the teeth of the comb and played "Dawn in an Old World Garden," with nightingale effects. He had memorized this song from hearing it so often on Muzak.

"You tried," the Nightingale said when he had finished. "But an imitation, however good, is nothing compared to the real thing." And there where she stood, in her gardening shoes, she sang a real nightingale song to prove it. Her song was beautiful beyond compare.

By request, the Goose then did a dance in her dancing shoes. At first, the Mother Quail was afraid this might be something wild. But it was a delicious tap dance called "La Tapioca." The little

Quails loved it and pretty soon were doing it as well as the Goose.

The paste diamonds in Gloria's slippers were quite thawed out now, and they caught the light of the moon when she kicked and pointed her toes. The first thing they knew, every bird in the store had fallen into step behind her.

"One thing I've found out about dancing shoes is that they can almost dance by themselves," remarked the Goose as she tapped right up the slope of the shoe stool and made a landing off the other side. The others all followed and did the same thing behind her. "Another thing I've learned is that once you start dancing, shoes stop hurting."

"La Tapioca" went into a snake dance. And when the Pigeon came snake-dancing in the opposite direction from everybody else and collided with the Crow, that's when they found he had his loafers on backwards.

"What a parade, all the same!" said the Pigeon. "I've seen a lot of parades in my time, but never one as good as ours. Never one as long or as slow or as loud or with me in it!"

The snake dance went into Pop-the-Whip, and the poor Hummingbird, who was by now at the tail end, was popped clear into the desk drawer and had to be fished out of a bed of paper clips by the Crane. She didn't mind. "On with the dance!" she said.

The Penguin started to soft-shoe in his saddle oxfords, and somersaulted again.

Then the Owl surprised the whole room by performing a very accomplished fandango. He seemed to lose ten years off his age before their eyes.

It might have gone on all night! Suppose Robbie Thompson had been awake and at the window of the store, looking inside as the moon was doing now! Well, he'd said "Shoes are for the birds!"

"Celebrations always make me cry," said the Whippoorwill finally. "I do want to be the first to break up the party. I'd better go now, back to my cheerless marsh."

"Why are you still so sad?" they asked.

But he did not tell. Shedding tears was an old habit with him. He may have forgotten the reason why, if he'd ever had one.

"Do you know what I think? I think you ought to be picked up and spanked," said the Mother Quail. "For being such a crybaby! And little as I am, I'll do it myself! Pay attention, children," she said to her forty-eight chicks.

And she swept up and spanked the Whippoorwill twenty-five or thirty times with her own brisk, whirring wings. Though she had to step out of her shoes to do it, she was a regular spanking machine.

"That's right," sobbed the Whippoorwill. "Whip poor Will!"

Arturo, always alert for what was needed, pointed out a convenient little door cut into the base of the big front door to the street, and they pushed him out.

"What comes next?" they cried. And the Robin asked, in particular, "What, and when, and where are the refreshments? Shall I go out and see what I can rustle up?"

"We can eat on the way home," said the Mother Quail. "Grasshoppers taste so much better in the open air. I think that before we leave, though, we ought to think of a parting gift for Mr. Friendly. I've heard so much about him tonight, I feel we know him as well as we now know the Parrot. Now what can we give him?"

"What about the wreath of bird's-foot violets, feathered carnations, eglantine, and seed pearls?" asked the Twelve-Wired Bird of Paradise. "I hate to see it go to waste."

"Mr. Friendly never wears wreaths," said Arturo. In this case, he was right about what Mr. Friendly wore. "But Miss Casey might find some use for it."

"Would he like a parting gift of shoes?" asked the Pigeon. "I could give him some loafers."

"If someone gives you a present, you can't give him the same present back," the Mother Quail pointed out. "That would be rude. Think of something better than that."

"I don't think anything can beat a golden egg," said the Goose. "And I always felt I could lay one, if I only had the encouragement."

"Well, why don't you lay one right now?" they said, encouraging her.

"Because I can think of an objection," she said. "A golden egg might embarrass Mr. Friendly. It would outshine *his* presents."

But the Parrot was rapping with his bill.

"Just a moment! *Presents*, did you say?" he called. "But Mr. Friendly's shoes aren't presents! In a store, you have to pay."

"Pay? What's pay?" cried the Goose. "I never paid for a

thing in my life.''

And ''What's pay?'' cheeped the Sparrows from down in their darkness.

''There are fourteen meanings in the dictionary, as I remember,'' said Arturo, ''but they all come to the same thing. 'Pay' is an old business word, and it's not altogether a happy word. It means nothing in the store is free.''

''I know what you're talking about,'' said the Park Pigeon. ''Popcorn! How much popcorn do you shell out, Parrot, to get us to wear the shoes out of the store?''

''I'm afraid you've got it backwards,'' said Arturo. ''The *customer* pays the *store,* not the other way round.''

''What kind of bird are you?'' exclaimed the Goose.

''I'm a shoe bird,'' Arturo replied. ''Not to be confused with a shoo-bird,'' he reminded them.

But they confused it at once.

''Shoo, then!'' they cried. ''Give us our shoes and shoo! Shoo, shoe bird, shoo!''

''Don't! Please don't!'' cried Arturo, holding on to the other birds, one after the other, by their tails. He was in danger of being shooed right out of The Friendly Shoe Store, by the little door.

''Let him stay,'' said the Goose. ''It's not his fault. If that's the way they do it in the shopping center, we'll pay. I'll pay for everybody!'' she cried. ''It will be my pleasure.''

''Do you carry a checkbook?'' asked Arturo, a little out of breath.

''No, but I wear a blue ribbon. I'm sure that's more becoming!'' she said gaily.

''If you pay, who'll be Miss Casey and take your payment at the cash stand?'' asked Arturo.

''Me, me, me!'' cried the Goose. ''I'll be Miss Casey too! I'll take it.''

''Now listen here, dear. Let *me* pay,'' said the Hen to the Goose. ''You ought to let another bird do something once in a while.''

''Certainly not,'' said the Goose. ''I want to be the one to do everything.''

And she ran forward on her high heels and once more caught the

revolving table. It was still going around, like a merry-go-round that never stops.

She was on top. There, with no more fuss than seemed right for the occasion, she laid an egg.

And there it was—a perfect egg, honest, timely, gracious, and original. It had an initial on it—a flowing "F" for "Friendly."

It didn't need to be golden—that might have been too much. It had a clear, lovely oval—as good an oval as the earth draws around the sun when it travels through spring and summer and fall and winter to bring the year to the full.

Every bird in the store—and there were some well-known layers there—admired the Goose's egg and said so. (Of course, it was unusually well set off by being laid on a revolving table.)

"I don't know what Mr. Friendly would say to that," Arturo said to himself. "But we can't correct it now. She's already laid it and it has Mr. Friendly's initial on it." And watching the egg go round and round and round, he added, "I think she's paid too much. But that's just like Gloria."

Then the Goose stepped down, tripped over to Miss Casey's cash register, and rang it up. With her golden toe she punched the number that she thought matched her egg, 0.

Ding!

"I did it!" she cried, overjoyed.

Her work had rung the bell.

7

"Is this the mysterious convocation of the birds?" asked a whisper from the dark outside.

"It's a surprise party—I think," answered Arturo.

"It's an Open House—I think," answered the Goose.

"It's a P.T.A. meeting—I think," answered the Mother Quail.

"It's a reunion—I think," answered the Dove.

"It's the parade," said the Pigeon. "And whoever you are, out there, you've missed it."

"I'm in the right place," said the voice. "I'd know my family anywhere by all the confusion." And a large bird, pale and sleepy-eyed, quite wingless, stepped in upon the window sill. They knew who she was, though they'd never seen her before—for who else could such a mysterious relative be? The Dodo.

Arturo said with a bow, "Madam Dodo, I'm sure I speak for every bird here when I say you are a surprise and also an honor to this occasion. Will you come the rest of the way in?"

"No, this is far enough, thank you," said the Dodo. She looked too distinguished, indeed, to step from the sill and get down on the floor with them.

The Crow was the only bird with nerve enough to approach her. He trotted right up in his basketball sneakers. "Madam Dodo, you've got the reputation of being extinct," he said.

"It is deserved. I *am* extinct," said the Dodo. "But when it was drawn to my attention that a mysterious convocation of all the birds had been called, I came anyway. Though no bird except the legendary Phoenix lives farther from here than I do."

"Mamma, are we extinct?" peeped the little Quails.

"Of course not," she said. "You'll go on forever. You're not extinct. Hush!''

"If I could rise to my office in Mr. Friendly's shoes, I'd look it up in my dictionary, under 'x'," said Arturo.

He didn't know that to find "extinct"—which means "to have come to an end"—he would need not only to fly in shoes but to look up the word under "e." All the same, he did well for a three-year-old Parrot. He listened.

"I'd be curious to know what made you extinct, Madam Dodo," said the Crow.

"First my curiosity went, then my wings," the Dodo said.

"Is that the whole story?" they asked.

"It's the heart of the story. Ah, the days when I used to feel curiosity, the days when I used to fly! They were one and the same."

"You have no wings at all now. How did you get here tonight, Madam Dodo?" asked the Crow.

"I got here without giving it a thought," the Dodo replied. "In my case, lack of curiosity can act very speedily indeed. It's the best way for a Dodo to travel. I expect to get home the same way. My, it's been a long time since I've seen my family! You're all very much like your great-great-great-great-grandparents."

"We're not a bit like our great-great-great-grandparents!" the Crow cawed. "There've been a lot of discoveries since your day, Madam Dodo! For one thing, old birds did nothing better than fly—but we young birds intend to walk! *We're* not going to spend the rest of *our* lives beating our wings against the air, when we could have our feet on solid ground! Do you know what we came here for tonight? Shoes!" said the Crow. "And we've got them! We tried them on, broke them in, and now they're even paid for, thanks to a silly Goose. Did you come for yours?"

"Not I," said the Dodo. "No indeed. I didn't come this long, long way to get shoes on my feet."

"What did you come for?" they all asked then. "Tell us."

"I came for love," the Dodo replied. "And to find that I'm remembered."

"So you may lose your wings and lose your curiosity, and still, after a thousand years, keep the hope of the love of your friends?" asked the Owl.

"I have what's more precious to a Dodo than hope—I have memory," she said. "I came for love because I remember so well what love is."

"We love you, Dodo!" called the birds in chorus.

"I'll remember that," the Dodo said. "Good-by."

"Wait!" they all cried.

"What for?" she asked.

"Wait because anything may happen next, in this strange and

marvelous world—maybe through the mistake of a Parrot, maybe through the wisdom of an Owl," said the Owl. "Birds may wear shoes and walk, and men may fly to the stars. But as even the Goose knows, there'll always be something to happen next! And we'll get busy about it."

"Do wait, Madam Dodo! The sun will come up. That's one thing that will happen," said the Lark.

"And we'll sing. That's one thing we'll get busy doing," promised the rest. "Wait for the songs!"

"That's the future," the Dodo pointed out. "When you're extinct, you don't think about the future. And you miss it. But you do think good and hard about *what lasts*. Will you remember the two things stronger than extinction?"

"One is love; the other is memory," they sang.

"And one is surprise!" Arturo cried before he knew it.

"But I no longer feel surprised, since my curiosity ran out," the Dodo sadly said. "Think of me as an hourglass that the sand has already run through."

"Oh, then what if we could turn you upside down?" asked the Woodpecker, who had a literal mind. "Would everything start over again?"

"I prefer to remain right side up, regardless of what may become of me," the Dodo said without hesitation. Then she yawned —a remarkable yawn that lasted as long as a sunset.

"If you won't wait for the party to be over, Madam Dodo, please take these beaded Indian moccasins with you as a special prize," the Goose said impulsively.

"Thank you, but I can't," said the Dodo. "I can get myself home, through exerting lack of curiosity, but not if I'm carrying a package." Her eyelids drooped. "Before you head for extinction, think it over!" she said. The next minute, her strong lack of curiosity had once more lifted her away, like a leaf on the wind.

"The Dodo's departure is her specialty. But it makes me wonder how *we'll* get out of here," remarked the Owl then.

"One thing sure, we can't leave by the way we came in," said the birds among themselves, looking up at the window. It was not a high window, really—until a bird looked up at it from the floor.

Then it seemed so high that it might have been a tree standing on top of a mountain.

"We're on our feet now, and our feet are right on the ground," said the birds, talking together.

"You can go out by the door marked Freddy," said Arturo.

He nodded toward the little door in the big door, which could swing from the top on its brass hinges.

"It looks rather small to me. Freddy must not be an Ostrich," said the Ostrich.

"He isn't," said Arturo.

At that moment came the smallest sound, just outside.

"That'll be Freddy now," said the Parrot.

"Freddy? Who's Freddy?" asked the others. "Freddy *Bird?*"

The little door swung inward from the night outside, and Freddy himself—as if he'd heard his name called—came walking in on four fur-clad feet.

8

Freddy was a black cat with black whiskers. As he stared with those green eyes of his, everything in the room turned green too—birds, shoes, even the moonlight. What eyes!

All the birds were screaming at once. "The Cat! The Cat!" they screamed. They screamed so loud and in such high treble that everything fell off the desk and out of the drawers, and even the Parrot's dictionary toppled right off the dictionary stand and fell from the cage to the carpet. "It's the Cat!"

"Well, isn't this Cat Night?" asked Freddy. His voice was baritone.

"It can't be. It's a bird family reunion," said the Mourning Dove. And she did sound forlorn!

"It's an Open House. And that's how *you* got in. Listen, Mr. Cat," hissed the Goose. "It was all simply splendid till suddenly you sneaked in on us!"

"And so it's a surprise party, after all, isn't it, Parrot?" asked the little Sparrows from deep in the shoe.

"No—it is Cat Night. I've just consulted the calendar," Arturo said. (The calendar had slid off the top of the desk and was now lying at his feet.) He turned and spoke quietly to the crowd of quaking birds. "This is Freddy, everybody. He's a roving janitor for the shopping center. And he's here right on schedule. This is his night to clean up in The Friendly Shoe Store. I hope he won't behave any worse than usual."

"Quick! Under my wings!" the Mother Quail cried. All forty-eight chicks obediently ran and clustered under her. They would have been perfectly hidden, too, except that now, all the way around her and pointing outward, were forty-eight pairs of little

brown school shoes.

"What's the matter? Not trying to run away, are you?" Freddy took a step toward them.

"Let's get out of here! Let's go!" screamed the Jay. "Go! Go!"

"But we can't!" the other birds screamed back.

"Why?" screamed the Jay. "Why? Why?"

"Can't get ourselves off the ground!"

Indeed, they seemed to be rooted to the carpet there in the green gaze of Freddy the Cat.

"Try! Try! Try!" yelled the Jay. He tried, himself, and it just didn't do any good. He couldn't rise an inch.

Then they all sang in despair, "No use! No use!"

"Then cry! Cry! Cry!" wailed the Jay.

They did cry. They cried with every cry and stutter and song and scream and mourning note and every hiss they knew. But from where they were—right down on the floor there—what fellow bird out in the world could ever hear them?

Then in flashed the Mockingbird through the window. For the moment, the others thought that help had come.

"Is this the bird's banquet?" he sang, doing some acrobatic

stunts in the air. "Sorry if I've kept you waiting. But I'm in a lot of demand as an after-dinner speaker, wit, and mimic, as you know."

"If you think this is after dinner, you're early," said the Robin bitterly. "Nobody's had a bite. And can't you see we're in terrible family trouble here?"

"What's going on?" exclaimed the Mockingbird. "I never saw birds so down in the dumps or looking quite so green."

"Look who's sitting on the shoe stool, in pouncing position," said the Owl. "To be brief about it: we've fallen into the toils of a Cat, with our shoes on. We can't rise an inch from the ground. Any moment may be our last."

"Ah! I've gotten here just at the psychological moment!" said the Mockingbird. "That's my favorite time to burst in."

"*I* was expecting you," said the Goose. "Those Western boots with silver spurs are for you. Put them on. And then see how scared *you'll* be!"

The Mockingbird put the Western boots on and looked terrified, for the moment.

"I just cleaned out the sardine department of the Super Supermarket and nipped over here to mop up a few mice," said Freddy in his rich baritone. "But it looks like a change in the menu for me tonight. I'll have bird and a cold saucer of sarsaparilla."

"Freddy!" gasped Arturo.

"And I see you've laid an egg for me, too, marked with an 'F,'" said Freddy. "I'll wait on it."

"Now I know!" screeched the Robin. "*We* are the refreshments!"

"Unless, by some miracle, we can get away first!" cried the rest. "But how?"

> "Heow, heow, heow, heow,
> Oh, heow will they ever get home?"

meowed Freddy, rolling those green eyes.

For a moment, not a bird could speak.

Then Arturo said, "The only way is to walk."

"Walk?" cried the other birds.

"We have to make our getaway on our feet?" the Hawk screamed out.

"Did you ever see a Hawk walk?" mocked the Mockingbird. He had recovered his mocking tongue. Though the psychological moment was his favorite time for arriving, that didn't mean he was a bit of help when he got there.

"So you're going to *walk* away from me?" growled Freddy. "For goodness' sake! Listen to me, my delicious little friends." And he opened still wider his green, green eyes, which gave such a different light from the lamplike eyes of the Owl. "Are you trying to insult me? May I ask you what joy and what pride a Cat could take in stalking a bird who could do nothing better than *walk?*"

"Yes, what a shocking word!" mocked the Mockingbird.

The Cat growled on. "Those look like Girl Scout shoes, little Miss Thrush. If I chased you in those, I'd have to pass you! I might end up in front and you a mile behind me!"

"Oh, don't paint such a picture!" wept the Song Thrush. And she told the others in short bursts of song, "The Cat is playing with us as he would a mouse."

"With you like this," said the Cat, "one swipe of my left paw would be all I'd need to catch every one of you. *It's too easy!* It's an insult to every ounce of my nature. Well, I won't play."

And Freddy began to wash himself, there on the shoe stool. He never glanced up, except occasionally into the mirror—as though nobody who mattered was there at all but himself and his reflection. He washed himself all over from one end to the other, and then looked at the birds, lazily, over his left hind leg raised in the air.

It was their turn to feel insulted now.

"The Cat doesn't *want* to catch us! He doesn't *want* to make a delicious meal of us!" cried the birds among themselves. "This is worse than ever!"

They threw paper clips at him, popped rubber bands, sailed the ash tray into his nose. They tried even a ball-point pen—three of them staggering under it together, driving it like a battering ram. Freddy never appeared to notice. His nose wasn't even dented.

And the Crow, with a yell, turned over the bottle of ink right on his head. But Freddy just sat there and absorbed it quietly—he was already as black as ink himself.

"I wash my hands of you birds," said Freddy. He walked over to the little door marked Freddy, curled up in a supercilious circle on the floor in front of it, and closed his eyes, all but two narrow slits.

The room darkened down. The moon was now under a cloud, too. And the Owl had shut his own eyes, the better to concentrate. In the quiet there came only the fluttering sound of pages turning. Arturo, who could read by the least possible light, was looking up "rescue" in the dictionary, starting at the front. (The Parrot had never had a chance to learn the alphabet.)

"In my opinion, the Cat's only pretending to be bored. But he's not," muttered the Owl. "I think he's biding his time."

"Did you ever hear an Owl growl?" mocked the Mockingbird.

While Arturo went flutter, flutter, flutter at the dictionary, all the other birds too (except the Mockingbird) were doing their own best to find a way out of this terrible situation.

Now the Swan came forward. She was mute, but in Swan sign language she asked them, "Are you all holding your breath? Here I go!"

And she rose to her toes, laced in their ballet slippers, and wildly drove herself straight through the air at the Cat!

Alas, she fell. Before all their eyes (and Freddy opened one of his, like a spotlight) she sank to the floor. The weight of her ballet slippers was too much for her. She came down in a graceful split, all right, but she couldn't get up. She lay there huddled and quivering.

"Are you hurt?" cried the Dove, pounding toward her in her nurse's shoes.

The Swan's wing was folded under her the wrong way. "But you don't really need it anyway," cooed the Dove.

"I'll be all right in a little while. Only my pride is really hurt," said the Swan in sign language.

"Follow me!" cried the Swallow next. "We'll scale the wall!"

He went creeping in his crepe soles up the wall toward the open window, but he'd crept only six inches when he slid back to the floor, giving an eerie cry.

"Did you ever hear a Swallow holler?" the Mockingbird mocked.

"The Mockingbird has changed sides—that's what he's done. He's on the Cat's side!" said the Mourning Dove. "That doesn't show much family feeling."

"I haven't any. I back the winner," he said. The psychological moment really brought out the worst in the Mockingbird.

"We shall have to crawl for it," said the Robin, weeping. "Like a worm!"

And the Mockingbird mocked, "Did you ever hear a Robin sobbing?"

But crawling like a worm was the hardest thing any bird ever tried in his life—surely much harder than it would have been for a worm to fly. Shoes did nothing but make it harder still. They had to give up crawling. And besides, waiting in front of that little door, marked Freddy, was Freddy.

"Well, now we've tried everything," said the birds in chorus. "Come on, eat us," they begged the Cat. "To keep us waiting is the cruelest thing of all."

"At least we die with our shoes on," said the Goose.

"*Now* the Whippoorwill has something to cry about! If only he knew the fate of all his friends," they said.

And then, from far off in the marshes, they did hear him cry: "Whip-poor-Will! Whip-poor-Will!"

"Still thinking of himself," said the Owl. "Well, he will be the last bird in the world. Maybe *that* will comfort him. In the flash of an eye, *we* shall all be only a memory in the mind of the Dodo. My, there's more than one kind of extinction."

"And Parrot, it's all your fault!" they screeched. "The Cat's going to catch us and clean our bones, and you're to blame!"

"Me?" cried Arturo. He'd just found "rescue" in the dictionary. There was only one meaning, and it was short: "to free."

"Yes, you're to blame!"

"You did call us here to be murdered, you know," said the Goose, looking up at him with reproachful eyes. "Though I am very glad we all got new shoes in the bargain."

And "Shoo!" they began at him once more. "Shoo! Shoo! Shoe bird, shoo!"

Arturo felt the dreaded word coming at him like a gale, and he had to hold onto the dictionary itself to keep from being blown clear away.

All of a sudden, he whipped around and sent that word back—straight at Freddy.

"Shoo, Freddy!" he yelled.

It was a clever idea—but the word didn't work on a cat. Freddy was impervious. He stayed put, licking his chops.

"Give up?" Freddy asked.

Arturo was now feverishly looking up "free" in the dictionary, starting from the back. And the example the dictionary gave was "free as a bird"!

"Well, I see it's up to me," said Arturo to himself now. "With some words, it's enough to know what they mean. With other words, you have to go ahead and *act* on what they mean. Well, I've got a beak I can count on. Thank goodness it's hinged! I can climb with it just as if I had an alpenstock. I can reach that window sill where I called, so lightheartedly this morning, and was heard by the Goose."

And he hooked his way up the wall. In his cloak of brilliant feathers he rose up the wall, inch by inch, by the power of his magnificent, hinged beak.

He reached the window sill. He stood on it. Then he yelled to all outdoors:

"Free the birds! Free the birds! To whom it may concern—help! May we expect a reply at your earliest convenience? Free the birds!" He yelled in all the languages he knew. And he knew Parrot, Patagonian, English, Pigeon, Pigeon-English, Commercial English, Goose and Latin.

All the night seemed to listen. And who answered his call?

This time, it was the Phoenix himself.

9

Out of that darkest moment, the store all at once grew colored like the east at sunrise. The Phoenix had flown down through the sky in his red plumes. Now he was lowering himself toward them on two powerful, gently moving wings, his eyes sparkling like rubies from his trip. He had come from the ends of the earth.

Alighting on the window sill, he opened his silvery beak and told them: ''You are all on the wrong track.''

The Parrot, the Peacock, the Twelve-Wired Bird of Paradise, and all the other bright birds were put in the shade by the presence of the Phoenix. He looked over all those birds there, at the Goose in her golden dancing slippers, the Owl in his Pullman slippers, the Robin in springy tennis shoes, the Mockingbird in boots and spurs, the Swan in ballet shoes, and the rest.

''How do we look?'' the Peacock couldn't keep from asking.

The Phoenix said to them all, ''You bring the tears to my eyes.''

''Bring the Phoenix a Kleenex,'' mocked the Mockingbird.

The Phoenix simply ignored him. He turned his rosy eyes on the Cat, instead—for of course he'd taken the situation in at a glance.

''Frederico,'' he said—for of course he knew even the full given name of the Cat—''retire.''

''Did you ever see a Cat scat?'' mocked the Mockingbird.

''Don't you mock *me*,'' said the Cat. And in the instant before he had to retire, he ate the Mockingbird, boot, bone, and spur.

Here was the family emergency the Dove had been waiting for— but she was too late to save the Mockingbird. She contented herself with stamping her foot in her nurse's shoe and saying, ''Good riddance!''

Then Freddy streamed toward the door with his name on it and

melted his own velvet black into the black velvet of night. And he stayed in complete retirement for twenty-four hours.

"Grandfather Phoenix," sang the birds, "you saved us from the Cat and the Mockingbird both. You freed the birds!"

"I was glad to do what I could," said the Phoènix. "Yes, I was able to save you from the Cat and the Mockingbird. It's true I know more than the Parrot, more than the Goose, the Pigeon, the Jay, and the rest of you, including the Owl; more than Robert Thompson in his sleep, and Jane awake; more than Mr. Frank Friendly, though he became a year older yesterday; more than his clerk, Mr. Claude Clark, and his stenographer-bookkeeper-cashier, Miss Camilla Casey; more than the Cat I have just put out; more than the Dodo, though she retains a remarkable memory. I know more about one thing, that is. *I know what my gift is.*"

"Your prize, do you mean, sir?" asked the Goose.

"Not prize—I never won anything in my life," said the Phoenix. "I mean my *gift.*"

"It's magic," said the Owl. "You are a magician, sir."

"Indeed I am," said the Phoenix. "But that's something like algebra. I took a thousand years off and learned it. But magic is not my gift. My born gift is your born gift, too. The most precious thing that belongs to me belongs to every bird down on that miserable floor."

"What is that, Grandfather?" they called up to him.

"How many grains of popcorn will it cost us to get that information from you?" asked the Pigeon. "Can't get something for nothing."

"Those who say *that* are apt to know very little about either something *or* nothing," the Phoenix firmly said. "It is possible to get something for nothing, and also something for something, nothing for something, and nothing for nothing. And to give it, too. There's more to everything than making a trade will tell you. Some things you can't buy. Some things you don't sell. Such as our born gifts." He looked at them hard. "These shoes have cost you too much," he said.

"But the Goose paid! She paid for everybody!" they all cried.

"Yes, she is a generous creature, who has laid here one of the best goose eggs I ever saw," said the Phoenix. "And how nice to have come from an egg," he added politely to them all.

"Doesn't the Phoenix come from an egg, Mamma?" whispered the little Quail chicks.

"No, he goes up in flames every five hundred years and arises again from his own ashes," whispered their mother hastily. "Don't interrupt him when he's speaking."

"But if you birds are going on the ground from now on," continued the Phoenix "you have *all* paid a fearfully high price for shoes!"

"Oh, Grandfather Phoenix, don't take my glory away," begged the Goose. "I thought I'd paid for everybody."

"You have *all* given up more than you seem to know," the Phoenix said. "Glory is a good word for it. But it's a *practical* glory. Don't stop to look 'practical' up now—you'll understand as we go along," he added kindly to Arturo.

"What glory have we given up? What can it be?" they asked one another.

"Does it begin with sssss?" asked the Goose.

"No, it ends with ssss," said the Phoenix. "All of you told me I'd freed you. But I haven't freed you—I can't. You have to free yourselves."

"But what with, sir? What with?" they cried.

"You must all be forgetting something. Will you remember if you look at me?"

And slowly the Phoenix unfolded before their eyes his splendid wings. They were like soft flames that leap as a signal from some cliff in the night sea, the feathers now beaded with starry dew. He lifted them till their tips met high above his crest.

"What do you see?" he asked.

"Grandfather Phoenix, *you're barefooted!*" they cried. Their eyes were all on his feet—his strange, pink, horny, naked feet with their ancient toenails like pink quartz. He was four hundred and ninety-five years old. "Where are your shoes?" they asked.

"You have forgotten!" he cried, and sang to them. "You and I, all birds alike, never allowed anything on earth to hold us down. What we have, let us keep. Let birds remember the feather! Or

we'll follow the Mockingbird down the throat of the Cat, or the Dodo down the wind to extinction.''

''Where are your *shoes*, Grandfather?'' cried the chorus of birds, led by the Oriole stubbornly warbling, ''Shoes, O shoes are for the birds, the birds, O, I say shoes are for the birds!''

''Oh, birds, think. Oh, birds, use the brains you have,'' the Phoenix implored.

And then Arturo spoke up—a little timidly, but he went bravely ahead. ''Grandfather Phoenix, it seems to me you're saying that even golden slippers with high heels and paste diamonds can never be as wonderful as the silliest Goose who puts them on.''

''That's me,'' said the Goose.

''That's very good, Arturo de la Patagonia,'' said the Phoenix, ''as far as it goes. Think harder. All birds have a gift they were born with. What is it?''

''Think for us, Grandfather! What is this gift? And how can we ever get home?'' the birds cried in one frantic chorus.

''*How did you get here?*'' the Phoenix softly said. ''In your own questions lie the answers.''

Then he rose up and off into the starry night, straight upwards with a soft rush of rosy air, up over the store and the park and the shopping center and the city and the river, and glowing like a comet he wound his way two or three times around the earth and then slowly receded from view.

''A bird can be *too* bright,'' said the Peacock, who had seldom

been so completely put into the shade.

But the Owl said, "Balderdash! No bird can ever be too bright. The Phoenix is out of our class, and let us be glad he looked in on us. Who remembers the last words he said?"

" 'How did you get here?' " the Parrot thoughtfully repeated.

"Well, I think I know. How did we get here? Why, by flying!" cried the Lark. "I came down from the very zenith! On my—"

"Wings!" shouted Arturo. "That's it! That's what the Phoenix was trying to make us say!"

"Wings!" said the Owl. "Fool that I nearly was, to forget. I should tie a string around my big toe to remind myself I have wings."

"Wings! Wings! I remember now as well as you do," said the little Wren. "Oh—to fly! Once more to stretch our wings and fly!"

"It comes back to me like an old song. Once we could all fly!" warbled the Oriole.

"Shall we rise like the Phoenix now?" cheeped the little Sparrows in their dark. "And fly up and away? And forget our overshoe?"

And they all sang, "Away! Away!" as Arturo, rushing everywhere at once, tapping them on their shoulders, the roots of their wings, said over and over, never to forget that word or its meaning again, "Wings, wings, wings, wings, wings!"

10

"Not so fast!" came a cawing sound. The Crow came striding out in front of them all in his basketball sneakers. "I'm not going to have a big shot like the Phoenix, or a has-been like the Dodo, or a brain like the Owl, or a wordy bird like the Parrot telling *me* what to do! Not a one of those birds is a Crow."

"Does that mean if they're for wings, you're not? Are you for shoes?" asked the Mother Quail. "Oh, maybe we can make it an educational meeting after all! We have something to vote on— wings or shoes!"

"Let's leave wings out of it, if you don't mind," cawed the Crow. "We'll vote on plain shoes. Are shoes for the birds? Yes or no. Every bird here has a voice in this, with a burst of song if he feels like it. And the first and loudest voice is mine: THE CROW SAYS NO."

"Wait! Who'll be the secretary and keep count of the votes?" interrupted the Mother Quail. "We ought to do it as much as possible like the P.T.A."

"I'll be the secretary," the Goose volunteered.

"No," said the Secretary Bird. "I'll be the secretary because I *am* the Secretary."

Stepping with one high step of her stiltlike legs onto Mr. Friendly's desk, she made a quick nest out of old bills, which she laced with twine and stuck together with Scotch tape and postage stamps. She settled in, and for each vote that came in she prepared to take out a quill from behind her ear and hold it up to be counted —for Yes in her left foot, for No in her right. Of course she had to take off her shoes first, and she set the little spike-heeled pumps on the desk just outside her nest.

"Ready!" she called. "Let's see how fast you can go."

"THE CROW SAYS NO!" yelled the Crow again.

"No shoes! No shoes! No shoes!" screamed the Jay. "Nay! Nay! Nay!"

"Make it more tuneful, more descriptive," chorused the others.

The Swallow twittered, "Going north in summer and south in winter—if we had to walk, we'd be late. Birds get there on time! So I say No Shoes."

"And when a fellow wants to migrate to the other side of the Big Drink, he'll run into other trouble if he walks," remarked the Tern. "Drowning trouble." He was a taciturn Tern, and this was his only remark all evening. "No Shoes."

"Four to nothing in favor of No Shoes," reported the Secretary Bird.

"When I spread my wings to cover my brood and their little shoes stick out, it gives the show away," said the Mother Quail. "I vote as a mother—No Shoes. My children vote the same."

"Fifty-three to nothing," said the Secretary Bird. She could pluck thirty-two quills a minute out of her head, which is not a bad speed.

Twenty Sparrows in a shoe voted as one and were counted as one. "No shoes!" they voted, and kept it up.

"Nobody looks at my tail any longer," the Peacock said. "They only ask to see my feet. I vote an indignant No."

"Shoes make a noise," said the Robin. "The most delicious worms, whose ears are also the sharpest, will hear me coming, tramp, tramp, tramp, and say to each other, 'I hear the step of the Robin! Dig in!' I vote No Shoes and oh, for a worm right now!"

"These loafers rest my toes," said the Pigeon. "But much as I enjoy creature comfort, I'm still fonder of picking up a little pop-corn in the park on a pleasant afternoon. I don't want to step on it. So I say No Shoes."

"Shoes are for the birds? O woeful, woeful words," mourned the Mourning Dove. "O no. O no. No."

"Fifty-seven to nothing in favor of No Shoes," reported their Secretary Bird. "I'm afraid the vote is not running very close."

"Will they take away our wings, to give us dusty clogs?" sang the passionate Nightingale. "No! No! Never, never! I'll sing myself to death in order to say— *No Shoes!*"

The Swan inclined her beautiful head and said in Swan sign language: "However the world may plead, I shall abandon my ballet shoes after tonight, and the applause and adulation of the public, to paddle along in secluded ways, feet naked in the stream —more beautiful above the waterline than anything else alive on land or sea."

"Let's see, is that vote *No*?" asked the Secretary Bird, with a frown on her downy forehead. The Swan gracefully bowed to agree.

"Wear shoes? Oh hush hush hush hush hush! Not in *my* bush," sang the Thrush.

"NO! NO! NO!" said the Crow again.

"Nay! Nay! Nay!" said the Jay again.

"Noo, noo, noo," said a little Scotch bird, a very small owl of Highland origin.

"Nix," whispered the Quail's forty-eight chicks, though the mother said, "If I hear another word of slang out of you, I'll tell the Eagle."

Through it all the Sparrows were constantly voting too.

"I'm getting a headache," said the Secretary Bird. "If you want me to keep count, would you mind voting one at a time and not more often than three times apiece? I would appreciate it."

"Now, I'm inclined to vote Yes," said the Hen, wandering about in her oxford ties. "And then I think, why not No? No, it's Yes. Yes, it's No."

"Make up your mind before you vote, please," begged the Secretary Bird. "I'm not here just to juggle my quills, you know."

"Eeny, meeny, miney, mo, I vote No," the Hen decided.

They took the doll shoes off the Owl's ears and sang into both of them, "Wake up and vote!"

> "Till shoes be made for Owls, with such a toe
> As Owls' toes be, be sure all Owls say No,"

said the Owl. Then he shook his head not only from side to side but also all the way around and back. (This was an optical illusion.)

"A hundred and thirty-one to nothing in favor of No Shoes," said the Secretary Bird. "Does any other bird want to vote before I close the polls? That will be in just a minute, because the quills of my head are numbered and I only have a hundred and thirty-four. There are three votes left, and one is mine." She drew out a quill carefully, like a lady taking out an important hairpin, and said, "It is my sincere pleasure and privilege to cast my vote at this time for No Shoes. And that makes it a hundred and thirty-two for No, zero for Yes."

"Now it's my turn!" said the Goose. She shook her blue ribbon straight and twinkled forward in her slippers. "I vote YES. And that makes it a tie."

"A tie?" cried the Secretary Bird. "Not according to *my* quills, and they're specially reliable because they grow so near the brain."

"Yes, it's a tie! That's what I say.

"And what can be the use
Of arguing with a Goose?"

sang the Goose, and danced some teasing steps.

"Suppose it *was* a tie," jeered the Crow. "You still can't come out the winner—there's nobody else on your side!"

"Don't be silly," said the Goose. "There's one more vote to come, and that's the Parrot's. And surely to goodness *he's* going to vote for shoes! Come on, Parrot! Vote!"

"I vote No Shoes," said Arturo quietly.

"No shoes! NO wins!" they shrieked and sang, all but the Goose.

"I can't believe it. After we've gone through all this together?" cried Gloria.

"I know I told *you* shoes were for the birds. But that was away back this morning," said Arturo. "I'm older now. So much has happened, Gloria."

"You'd vote against your old friend, in her first pair of golden slippers?" she reproached him. "After I was Mr. Clark? After I was Miss Casey? After I paid? I don't know what you'd have done without me this evening!"

And certainly, she was very much of a goose—but that had never kept her from being kind, and Arturo knew it.

"I'm sorry, Gloria," he said. "I do like you. But my vote's still No."

"Just a second," said the Secretary Bird. She was frowning again. "I'm afraid that throws me off, Mr. Parrot. I'd already put your quill in my other foot, you see. I was as sure as the Goose was that you'd vote for your own shoes. So I think you'll have to change your vote. That's easier on me than having to shift my quill, and just as the polls are closing."

"I vote No Shoes every time!" Arturo exclaimed. "Even if it throws the Secretary Bird into a secretarial frenzy! I know how I'm voting! I've got a mind of my own! Just since this morning," he added.

"Stop worrying, everybody," said the Goose. "What does it matter who wins the vote? We've got the shoes!" And she spun around on her toes.

"Yes, voting against them afterwards was no use," said the Owl.

"It's too late," said the Mourning Dove. "Too late! Too, too late!—Won't everyone sadly join in?"

"Too late!" repeated Arturo.

And the rest of them looked at him hard, all the birds, and said, "It's your fault. You thought up the whole idea. We owe all our troubles to you!"

"It seems so recent that I was the hero," said Arturo sadly.

"And I make a motion that a spanker be appointed," said the Mother Quail. This was seconded forty-eight times by her own children.

But the Owl said, "Let's give him something more lasting. A spanking happens, it's over and forgotten. Can any bird here think of anything that's permanent?"

"Love and memory," whispered Arturo. "But of course those aren't punishments—they're just the opposite. They won't give those to me."

"A statue in the park is pretty permanent," said the Park Pigeon. "Let's have a statue of the Parrot. And Pigeons will sit on it without the slightest regard for ever and a day."

"Yes, that's called Oblivion," said the Owl. "That's more lasting than a spanking, but it's beyond our means."

"Just so they don't shoo me," whispered the Parrot to himself. "To me, that's the worst."

"Name the day after him," the Mother Quail now suggested. "It would give our children a date to memorize in Bird History, and they would get it on their exams. Question: When is the worst day in Bird History and why? Answer: The worst day in Bird History is the first beautiful day in September when the feel of fall is in the air, because that's when birds were first shackled in shoes. It's called Black Parrot Day. Every year, when Black Parrot Day rolls around, the birds trudge back to the same spot, The Friendly Shoe Store, and celebrate as best they can while their hearts are heavy as their feet."

"How do they celebrate?" Arturo asked.

"By shooing the Parrot," she replied, and he groaned.

"I don't wholly deserve it," said Arturo. "When I was too young to think for myself, I repeated some words of Robbie Thompson's."

"What branch of the Robins is that?" asked the Robin sharply.

"No kin to you. Robbie Thompson is a little boy and a friend of mine," Arturo said. "He meant no harm, of course. He may only have been repeating what somebody told *him!*"

"Then he's a parrot," said the Robin. And most of them agreed.

"I repeated Robbie's five little words out the window, there—I didn't stop to think what would happen," said Arturo. "We all carried Robbie's idea out. We followed his suggestion through. All the way."

(Robbie Thompson, if he'd been waked up at that moment and asked about this, would have said: "But what I said was a joke! Everybody was supposed to laugh! I bet if he'd heard me, even my father would have laughed!" Yet his explanation wouldn't have helped the birds, for birds never laugh and never will laugh. Wonderful as it is to have wings and fly, and wonderful as it is to laugh, for some reason nothing that flies has ever laughed, and nothing that laughs has ever been given wings. Each has his own gift.)

"I listened to Robbie Thompson," said Arturo. "And my motto was: If you hear it, tell it. So what followed was bound to happen."

"He ought to be spanked, and you ought to change your motto," said the Mother Quail.

"Too late, too late," the Mourning Dove mourned on.

"It isn't too late for changing your motto," the Owl said now to Arturo. "It isn't too late for anything, if you knew much about lateness." He flooded them all with his yellow stare, and continued: "To say you've made a ridiculous mistake and correct it, it's never too late. What about the hour before dawn? That's a good time. It's the best hour of the twenty-four, to me. And that's what it is right now."

"I see now that 'If you hear it, tell it' is a motto for very young Parrots only," said Arturo. " 'If you hear it, think it over.' That's better."

"Do I hear a motion to make it unanimous that shoes for the birds are a ridiculous mistake?" asked the Mother Quail.

"What's unanimous?" asked forty-eight little voices at once, the Quail chicks.

"You are," said the Owl.

Arturo, after he'd consulted the dictionary, told them kindly, "It means that in at least one thing, everybody feels alike. All right," he told them all, "if I see Robbie Thompson one of these days, I could hop on his shoulder and give his discovery back to him!"

"Give the discovery right back to Robbie Thompson!" they cried in full chorus. "That's what you can do with it! That's brilliant! Parrot, you're getting brilliant!"

"No, just improving," said Arturo. But it felt very good to be getting a compliment again.

"And what will we do with the shoes?" asked the Mother Quail. "I've got forty-nine pairs right here in my own little family."

"The shoes can all be returned to Mr. Friendly and go back on his shelves where they belong—somehow," said Arturo. "He's very fond of the merchandise."

"The rest of you can give back your shoes if you want to," said Gloria now. "But not me! Gold shoes are what I can't live without!"

"Dear Goose," said the Owl, "is there a chance that you, like the Parrot, may learn more on your birthday?"

"Nonsense! I don't have birthdays!" teased the Goose.

"May I just try and see if reason will persuade you?" asked the Owl. "That's all that's left. Goose, if we wear shoes, we'll have to give up flying."

"That's all right with me, just so I can get over the Thompsons' fence. I'm the domestic kind," said Gloria. "And I want my gold shoes."

"Well, then," said the Owl, "if you paid any attention to the Dodo, you'd know how sorry you'd be to be extinct."

"Whatever it is, it sounds a long way off," said Gloria.

"I'm afraid that when the Phoenix was speaking with his silvery tongue, you weren't listening," said the Owl.

"What Phoenix?" she said. Some birds' memories are even shorter than ours. "Anyway, I expect he was a pretty old Phoenix, and I'm still a young Goose. And I want my gold shoes."

"Then listen to this: To have wings and not fly is a perfect disgrace," said the Owl. "As was proven when the Cat couldn't stomach more than one of us."

"Well, but the best part of the whole party was what happened to the Mockingbird," said the Blue Jay.

"And I don't know the meaning of disgrace," said the Goose.

"So, Goose, do you want birds to be disgraceful, extinct, and walking around in all the danger of the ground?" the Owl cried.

"All I know is I'm happy in golden shoes," said the Goose.

The Owl threw up his wings in despair. "Parrot! You have the gift of the gab," he said. "You talked the Goose into wearing shoes. Now talk her out of it. As long as even one bird keeps wearing shoes, the rest of us will be uneasy."

"Will nothing change your mind?" Arturo asked the Goose.

"Nothing ever has," she replied.

"But tonight I've learned you *have* to be able to change your mind, now and then, and on some matters," said Arturo. "Speaking only of cats, I've had to change my mind about Freddy. As I read in my office and watched him go about his work on Cat Night, I always thought he was a simple, affable, purring sort of cat, with nothing on his mind but mice."

"And what about your opinion of owls?" said the Owl. "You must have been in awe of my brains, up to now. Tonight you discovered what a really nice Owl I am—easy to talk to and easy to get along with, on the whole."

"Well, I think I've learned something a little new about every bird tonight," said the Parrot. "And about me too."

"You all think you're so smart!" the Goose exclaimed. "Stop bragging. You aren't the only birds in the world! You're only the pick, as I happen to know—I sent the invitations! What about the rank and file? They'd want me to have my golden shoes!"

"We have not heard from the rank and file," said the Secretary Bird.

"No news is good news," said the Goose. "They're on my side."

Just then, the Carrier Pigeon flew in through the window.

"My! It's still a long way around the world, no matter what they do to improve it," he said, out of breath. "I picked up a new message on the way back. Do you want to hear it? As a matter of fact, it's for you. Listen. *An astronomical proportion of absentee birds casts its vote for No Shoes.* Want me to interpret it? The rank and file say NO!"

"It's only because they weren't invited!" wailed the Goose.

"Hooray!" the rest of the birds were calling. "We all agree, all agree but a Goose! Hooray for the ones who weren't invited! Hooray for the ones who were! And once more, hooray! hooray! hooray! for ourselves!"

"Isn't that the note to go home on?" asked the Swallow.

"Yes, that's the word on which to disband a meeting," said the Mother Quail.

"There are still a few details," said the Parrot. "Like tidying up, you know, and returning the shoes. The Friendly Shoe Store opens for business at 8 A.M."

The Hen went over the floor quickly, sweeping with her wings; then the Turkey dusted. The Crane speared up all the loose tissue paper on his long, sharp bill. Then he didn't know where to put it. The Parrot had to explain to him about the wastebasket.The Goose stood by and let others do the cleaning up, because, after all, there she was in golden slippers.

They hung the wreath on the back of Miss Casey's chair where she couldn't miss it.

"I feel almost as if we knew Mr. Friendly," said the Secretary Bird. "I think we should write him a note of thanks for the use of his store and leave it on his desk. And I ought to be able to write it."

She seized one of her ever-ready quills (which happily wrote without being dipped in ink, like a ball-point pen), took a sheet of paper from her nest, and scratched rapidly across it. She blotted it with her breast. The result looked more like "Thank you" than what some people are able to write. All the birds admired it. The Flicker, with an unexpected burst of approval, notarized it with his red seal.

And at that moment came cockcrow.

11

"I must run," said the Hen.

"We must all *fly!*" they sang.

"Take it easy! Don't get excited," cried Arturo to them all. "Just walk through the little door in the big door, out onto the doorstep under the sky, and wait for my signal."

So the party began to break up.

"Heavens! I do look a wreck," said the Secretary Bird. Pausing in front of the floor mirror, she set all her quills back in at becoming angles.

They all said good-by to the Goose.

"It was a good parade," said the Pigeon. "Backwards or forwards or any way you want to look at it."

"You'd have been sorry if you'd gone to the library instead," said the Goose graciously.

"This is the first time I've ever been to a bird party on Cat Night," said the Mourning Dove, "except in dreams."

"I'm glad you were able to come *and* able to leave," said the Goose. "It's nice to be still alive when it's time for the sun to come up."

"Next time you ask us, give a little more thought to refreshments," said the Robin.

"At least *we* weren't eaten," said the Goose graciously. "That's something."

"And you got the only pair of gold slippers in The Friendly Shoe Store!" said the Twelve-Wired Bird of Paradise. "No wonder you hung onto them. I may find some somewhere else. Where is The Unfriendly Shoe Store?"

"Perhaps that's the name of the chain store down the street," said the Goose kindly. "If you find golden slippers for yourself, the Goose and the Bird of Paradise will be twins."

"It must have been an interesting party," said the Carrier Pigeon. "I enjoyed carrying the invitations and having some small part in breaking it up."

"Well, at least I won't have to go back to the desert and be an ostracized Ostrich," the Ostrich said. "I would never have lived it down if I'd had to wear overshoes home. In just a few minutes I'll be leaving them behind."

"It must have been educational," the Mother Quail said. "But I'm afraid my children didn't learn anything that they didn't know already, and eleven of them went to sleep."

"I stayed wide awake and I learned plenty," her eldest chick said, and recited in a clear voice, "Use your wings, give your best, and remember the love of friends. And shoes may come and shoes may go, but Quails go on forever."

"That's pretty good, little fellow," said the Owl. "Well, shall I sum up the evening?" he asked as he shouldered his way toward the little door in the big door. "I would say it was partly wise, partly ridiculous, partly sad, partly delicious, partly dangerous. How full of mistaken ideas is the average bird! No telling what foolishness they'd have got into without me!"

"I'm glad we got into exactly the foolishness we managed to get into *with* you," the Goose assured him. "To me, it was perfect foolishness."

The Robin, as he said good night, dived playfully at the Goose's shoe and carried off one of the diamonds. He went through the little door, and on the doorsill he cracked and ate it.

"It's not sugar inside." That's as much as he told them.

Then the whole crowd was through the door, waiting on the door-step.

"Now," said Arturo. "Shoes are hard to put on. But they take off—like this! So easily, really," and he stepped out of his. "Presto!"

"Well done," said the Owl. "A beautifully simple solution!"

"It won't be so easy for every bird," said Arturo. "But don't worry. When I give the signal word, rise. Dangle your feet. And up in sweet air, your shoes will fall off by themselves. Most things are easy at the last.''

''And you're staying behind?'' they sang.

''If it wouldn't be unbusinslike, I'd go with you,'' Arturo confessed, for he had a little thought of Patagonia, where even the night sky was as blue as the skin of a plum, and the bananas were as bright as the moon. ''I'd like to fly back to see my mother. By now she's old and may have faded. For one thing, she could tell me for sure if I haven't had a birthday this evening.''

''Yes, fly with us,'' they sang. ''There's nothing holding you— not a shackle, not a shoe.''

''But what would Mr. Friendly do without me!'' he said.

So they sang him a song, ''Poor Little Patagonian,'' in which strains of pity, envy, affection, and an impatience to take off their

shoes at last were delicately blended.

And so he gave them the signal. Very softly, very affectionately, he said, "Shoo...." And they gently rose.

For though words have strong meanings, so much does depend on the way they are said.

As the birds began rising, they shed their shoes from their feet. Some fell off right away; some took a little while to come loose. All the birds cast loose their shoes like tiny sandbags. The overshoes, the basketball sneakers, the school shoes, the ballet shoes, the Pullman slippers and doll shoes, the loafers, and all the rest drifted down like the early autumn leaves, or like little letters sent on their way. Exactly like little letters that are being delivered to their right address, they slipped through the letter slot in The Friendly Shoe Store's front door and landed safe inside, on the mat that said "Welcome."

The sun was just coming up. And today, once again, the birds soared free. As they rose, they sang. The streams of birds lifted and spread over the sky, like the opened wings of the Phoenix, then parted and took their separate ways, each bird for home.

"Well, birds are back on the wing," said Arturo from the window sill where he watched them off.

Back in the store, he did a last-minute chore: he drew the tacks from the Sale signs and put them back into their drawer. At once, the shoes, no longer reduced, began to get bigger. Soon they reached very nearly the same size they'd been to start with. A few, however, did pinch some toes a little, forever after. And their wearers never knew why.

Only the Goose had not gone home. She was still too excited.

"Now I'm going to take forty winks myself," Arturo told her. "I work, you know. It'll soon be time for Mr. Friendly to open up, and I'll have to be right on the job."

"Do you know," the Goose exclaimed, "these faithful golden slippers of mine still feel wonderful, though they must be nearly worn out. I haven't had such an exciting time since the night I was the Grand Prize at the Supermarket!"

"Then hoping to serve you again at some not too distant date, I beg to remain most faithfully yours," said Arturo. He was really talking in his sleep. That was the way Mr. Friendly ended his business letters when he dictated. So the Goose took the hint and tiptoed out through Freddy's door.

Then Arturo closed his dictionary, and flew with it up to its stand. He drew the curtains around his cage, which made it his private office. He wet his throat with a sip of buttermilk, dropped onto his perch, and slept.

In her golden slippers the Goose walked home. She could still fly over her own fence. That was as much as she cared to fly. In a moment she was in her own back yard.

Robbie's father, Mr. Thompson, who was just out of bed, had stepped to the door to pick up the morning paper. When he saw the shoes his wife had told him about (for tomorrow was *her* birthday) come walking home on Jane's goose, he stepped inside, shut the door, and burst out laughing.

And Gloria, as the sun came up, was plucking and eating a tender slip of grass in her golden bill.

12

"Good morning, Arturo," said Mr. Friendly when he arrived at the store at eight o'clock. "Is everything under control?"

"Yes, sir, everything's under control," said Arturo. "I was on the job."

"From the looks of things, Freddy's been here again," said Mr. Friendly.

"I'll try to give you a report of what happened during the night, sir," began Arturo.

"No, I leave all the night work to you," said Mr. Friendly. "And I'm sure there's some very simple explanation for all the shoes being on the welcome mat this morning."

"There is an explanation, but it may not be simple," said Arturo.

"Then don't bother me with it," said Mr. Friendly. "The day-time business is enough for me, and of course I trust you absolutely."

Mr. Clark, who had all the shoes to put back into the right boxes and all the boxes to put back onto the right shelves, said as he ran up the ladder, "There's not a mark or a scratch on any of these shoes, or any visible signs of wear."

"Good," said Mr. Friendly. "Well, everything's well under control."

"All but the golden slippers, sir," said Arturo. "They're gone for good, I think. Shall I tell you how?"

"Arturo, those shoes were for demonstration purposes only," said Mr. Friendly. "They were made of cardboard, so don't worry. But there's something in their place on the revolving table. What is it, a new-laid egg?"

The Parrot brought Mr. Friendly his spectacles and helped to

fix them straight on his nose. Mr. Friendly leaned down and took a closer look at the egg and said, "It *is* new-laid. Almost certainly by a goose. I wonder who it's for?"

"Mr. Friendly, that goose egg has your initial on it," said Miss Casey, who had keen sight.

"So the egg's for me? Well, I think I deserve it," said Mr. Friendly. "Is there any mail?"

Miss Casey brought him the note the Secretary Bird had left behind on the desk. "This must have come by special delivery," she said.

"It's not written on the typewriter," said Mr. Friendly. "I can't quite read it."

"It says 'Thank you,' " said Arturo.

"I wonder what for!" said Mr. Friendly. "How very kind! Well, this certainly is an unusual morning. Arturo, I know this much: you deserve a bonus," he told the Parrot. "So I'm giving you a two weeks' vacation with expenses paid. You'll have enough time even to fly home to Patagonia, if you'd like to surprise your mother. But be sure to come back."

"Thank you, Mr. Friendly!" cried Arturo. He had wondered if, when Mr. Friendly came in this morning and found everything so safe and sound, he might raise his salary from buttermilk and crackers to watercress sandwiches, bananas, and sassafras tea, plus the combination that opened the refrigerator door. "But this is ten times more wonderful!" he said to himself.

"Start any time you want to," said Mr. Friendly.

"I'll wait till the school rush is over," said Arturo.

He knew that Mr. Friendly could spare him better after that. He remembered, too, that he had a little business of his own with Robbie Thompson.

When Miss Casey found the wreath left by the Twelve-Wired Bird of Paradise, she exclaimed, "Oh! Just what I've been looking for! If nobody comes to claim this wreath by 5 P.M., it's mine."

(She liked it so well that one day in the future she decided to get married in it. And after the wedding—she married Mr. Clark—she forgot office worries completely. But up until then, she did worry about that pair of golden slippers changing into a goose egg.)

"The surprise of my life was when I found myself learning, instead of repeating," said Arturo now to himself. "Of course, it took something a little unusual to get me started. But after that surprise party, I believe I can keep my head about anything—and not have to bother the Phoenix again to come to my assistance. In my questions lie the answers. After all, it must be nearly time for the Phoenix to concentrate on rising from his own ashes. Everybody has a birthday coming! And even on the day he's five hundred again, the Phoenix still may have something left to learn. There does seem to be a whole lot!"

"What was that?" asked Mr. Friendly.

For the Parrot had not said one word of this in Commercial English. Nor was it in English at all. The time comes when every living creature thinks certain thoughts to himself in the language, whatever it is, that is nearest his own heart.

"It was nothing about shoes, Mr. Friendly," said Arturo. "I was just thinking about life in general. But here's our first customer of the day!"

And as Mr. Friendly came forward to say, "Good morning!" Arturo dutifully clacked his bill like a door knocker. He was back on the job.